MURDER AT THE CATHEDRAL

AN EXHAM-ON-SEA MYSTERY

FRANCES EVESHAM

Boldwood

First published in Great Britain in 2020 by Boldwood Books Ltd.

Cover Design by Nick Castle Design

The characters and events described in the Exham on Sea Mysteries are all entirely fictitious. Some landmarks may strike fellow residents of Somerset, and particularly of Burnham on Sea, as familiar, although liberties have been taken with a few locations.

A CIP catalogue record for this book is available from the British Library.

Paperback ISBN 978-1-80048-023-0

Large Print ISBN 978-1-80048-024-7

Ebook ISBN 978-1-80048-026-1

Kindle ISBN 978-1-80048-025-4

Boldwood Books Ltd
23 Bowerdean Street
London SW6 3TN
www.boldwoodbooks.com

1

Libby Forest and the enormous sheepdog, Bear, climbed the steep street to Wells Cathedral. With no cats to chase, Bear turned his attention to the human passers-by and tried to plant a slobbery, doggy kiss on each face. Libby's cheeks flamed with embarrassment as she steered the animal through Penniless Porch, the archway leading to the green lawn in front of the cathedral. 'I almost wish I hadn't agreed to look after you. The sooner Max gets home and takes you back, the better.' No need to tell Bear how much she loved having him with her as she visited the beauty spots of Somerset.

The duo of walkers paused at last, Libby's eyes drawn to the statues carved on the building's stunning West Front. She raised a warning finger at the wriggling dog. 'You're on your best behaviour.' The last thing she needed was a spat with Louis, the cathedral cat, and there was nothing Bear enjoyed more than chasing cats. He made an exception only for Fuzzy, Libby's aloof marmalade cat, who'd turned out to be Bear's soulmate. The pair liked curling up together in as small a space as possible and dozing the hours away.

They navigated the spiral stairs to the café without incident and Libby poked her head round the door. Conversations buzzed amid enticing smells of cake and spice, but Libby was immune to food. Cakes and chocolates were her business, and she spent most days mixing and tasting, surrounded by sugar. On a rare free morning she stuck to coffee.

She spotted Angela Miles at once. Immaculate grey locks teased into a neat French Pleat, pearl earrings dangling from tiny ears, her friend raised a leather-gloved hand in welcome. Libby tugged at her thatch of damp brown hair. She should have visited the hairdresser weeks ago.

Pulling a dog treat from the jumble in a pocket of her parka, she bribed Bear to lie down under the table. Angela stirred a steaming cup of coffee. 'So, your son's getting married in the cathedral? How wonderful.'

'Isn't it? His fiancée, Sarah, has family connections; her mother grew up two streets away. Even so, they were lucky to find a vacant date for the wedding. The cathedral gets booked up in the summer, but there's a cancellation in June. At least the weather will be warmer. I'm tired of winter...'

Angela's attention had drifted. Libby, intrigued, followed the direction of her friend's gaze. A familiar figure occupied a table in the corner with her back to the room. Even at a distance, the back-combed haystack of black hair was unmistakable. Libby would recognise Mandy, her lodger and apprentice, anywhere.

She rose to wave. 'Hey, Mandy...'

Angela tugged her arm. 'Shh. Don't interrupt. Mandy hasn't seen us and she's having a row with Steve.'

That young man, Angela's nephew and Mandy's boyfriend, sported spiky, dyed-black hair and a tight t-shirt. He banged a fork on the table. 'Suit yourself,' he snapped, face red and angry.

Libby's eyes met Angela's. 'We shouldn't eavesdrop.' They

turned away, full of good intentions, trying to carry on a conversation, but the fight proved irresistible. At last, they gave themselves up to unashamed eavesdropping.

Steve's romance with Mandy had lasted almost a year, even surviving his move from Wells Cathedral School to study music at the Royal College of Music in London, but the relationship looked under strain, today.

Libby caught fragments of angry whispers. 'You could if you wanted to,' Steve hissed.

Mandy wailed, 'You don't even try to understand…'

To Libby's disappointment, she missed the rest and, succumbing to guilt, dragged her attention back to the reason she and Angela had arranged to meet. From the depths of her bag she retrieved sketches for the bride's wedding dress, samples of lace, and lists of guests. 'She hasn't made her mind up yet, so people can see the sketches – apart from Robert, of course. Sarah tells me it's unlucky for the groom to see the dress before the wedding.'

Angela settled a pair of reading glasses on her nose, leaned both elbows on the table and examined the plans, cooing with approval. 'What a gorgeous dress. I love a fishtail, don't you? Sarah will look stunning.'

She sat back. 'Now, tell me about the cake. That's your department, isn't it? What are you going to make? Sponge cake? Fruit? How many tiers? I bet you can't wait to start.'

Libby avoided her friend's eye. 'They want cheese.'

'Cheesecake? That's unusual, but I suppose you could make it look good—'

'Not cheesecake. Cheese. Three different varieties, all produced in Somerset. Cheddar, Brie and – er – Buffalo. One for each layer of the cake. Sarah's father's a dairy farmer.'

Angela's eyes opened wide. 'So, you won't be icing the biggest and best wedding cake in Somerset, after all?'

'No; and I had such plans…'

Their laughter died as Mandy's voice rose. 'Don't you dare call me a stupid child. I've got, like, a job, you know. I can't come running down to London every time you snap your fingers. Why don't you ask your friend, Alice. She'll be there in a second.'

A hush fell throughout the café, half embarrassed and half expectant. Mandy threw a handful of coins on the table and stamped out. Steve scrambled to his feet as if to give chase, but stopped, hesitated as though making his mind up, and flopped back into the chair.

Angela peered over the rim of her reading glasses, muttering under her breath, 'Follow her, Steve, you idiot,' but the young man sipped coffee, as though quite unaware he was the centre of attention. Only a spot of pink on each cheek gave the game away.

Angela sighed. 'That'll teach me to eavesdrop. I was hoping they'd stay together for good and maybe even get married. I know they're young, but they seemed so happy.'

Libby sorted the wedding plans into a pile. 'D'you think that's the end of the relationship? Perhaps they're not as well suited as we thought.' Mandy had seemed to be on cloud nine recently. 'It's a shame, but they're still young. Living so far from each other must be a strain.'

She put her papers back in the bag. 'I remember Alice. I met her one day at your house. Very glamorous and a musician, like Steve.' She shrugged. 'Maybe she's a better match for him, but I'm sorry for Mandy. It seems her heart's about to be broken.'

Angela rearranged packets of sugar in the flower-painted china container. 'Look at us, worrying about Steve and Mandy as if they're our children.'

'Mandy's almost a third child to me, now Ali and Robert have grown up and left home. She's tidier around the house than they ever were, though.'

Angela looked thoughtful. 'I never had children of my own. Didn't think I had maternal instincts until Steve's motorbike accident. That hit me for six.'

'You were like a tiger with her cub,' Libby recalled, 'and you spent every day at the hospital until you were certain he'd recover.'

Angela laughed. 'I suppose you never stop wanting to look after them, do you? No matter how old they are.'

The excitement died away, the café returned to its normal state of soporific calm, and Bear rested his head on Libby's lap, eyes pleading for treats. As she tickled his favourite spot, just behind a front leg, Angela's phone rang.

She made an apologetic face. 'Sorry, do you mind if I take it? It's the verger. I expect he's calling about my shift this afternoon.' Angela worked in the cathedral as a volunteer guide.

She answered the phone with a cheery 'Hello,' but a second later, the smile froze on her face. Colour drained from both cheeks, leaving Angela looking pale and shocked. Her lips moved, but no sound came. Her eyes flickered.

Libby put out a hand, afraid her friend was about to faint, but Angela recovered enough to talk. 'Are you sure? It can't be true – I mean – it was only yesterday...'

Her hand shook and the phone fell, spinning and rattling, onto the floor.

'Is everything OK?' Libby bit her lip at such crassness. What a stupid thing to say when it was blindingly obvious things were very far from OK.

Angela was mumbling, shaking her head. 'It's dreadful. I can't believe it...' She gasped for air.

Libby squeezed her elbow. 'Breathe out, now. Slowly.' Angela shuddered, regaining control. 'That's better. Now, tell me. What's happened?'

'It's Giles – Giles Temple – he's been working at the cathedral library.' Libby had never met Mr Temple, but Angela had spoken of him once or twice. Whenever she mentioned his name, her cheeks turned a delicate shade of pink.

'What about him?'

'He's – he's had an accident.'

'Is it serious?'

Angela nodded, lips quivering. 'Very. I'm afraid he's dead.'

2

LIBRARIAN

'Is your friend ill?' One of the women serving at the counter
hurried across the room, sympathy in her eyes.

'She's had a nasty shock.' Libby avoided going into details.
Soon enough, everyone working in the cathedral would know
about Giles Temple's death.

'Well, she'd better have a cup of tea, that's my advice. It's the
best remedy for shock. Poor Mrs Miles. I've seen her many time,
working in the cathedral. Very kind, she is. Couldn't be nicer. No
airs and graces, like some folks working at the cathedral.'

The woman bustled about, bringing a pot and cups on a tray.
Libby, with superhuman self-control, asked no questions of
Angela as she poured tea, added milk and several spoons of sugar,
and waited until her friend drank every drop.

As Angela settled the empty cup back in its saucer, hands still
shaking, a touch of colour returned to her cheeks. The threat of a
fainting fit gradually receded, and Libby gave way to curiosity.
'Now, give me the facts. What happened?'

'The librarian found Giles this morning when he opened the

room. He'd been—' Angela swallowed and finished in a rush, 'He'd been strangled. With a chain.'

'Strangled? You mean, accidentally?' Not another suspicious death in Somerset, surely. 'What do you mean by a chain? Some sort of necklace?'

Angela shook her head, as though trying to clear it. 'No, it's a chained library, you see. The chains are attached to valuable books and bolted to the shelves to prevent anyone wandering off with a priceless volume. So many books in the library are irreplaceable.'

Her high-pitched laugh sounded dangerously close to hysteria.

Libby concentrated, determined not to miss a single word as Angela explained. 'There are keys, you see. One locks the gate to the library, and another attaches each chain to a book.'

Tears glittered in Angela's eyes. Libby, horrified as she was, couldn't help a familiar spasm of excitement in her stomach. She felt it at the beginning of each of her amateur investigations, and every time she'd succeeded in uncovering the criminal. 'And one of the chains was used to strangle the victim?' Libby winced as the shocking image took shape in her head.

'Apparently. It happened last night. Giles was working late; he often did...' Angela picked at a tissue, pulling it to shreds.

Libby sipped the dregs of cold tea left in her cup, trying to make sense of the information. 'Are all the books chained?'

'Only those from before the eighteenth century.' Talking about the details of the library arrangements had a calming effect on Angela, so Libby let her talk. At least her teeth had stopped chattering. 'You know, early copies of the King James version of the Bible, illuminated manuscripts from the sixteenth century, books of maps, translations of religious books into different languages. All that sort of thing...'

Angela screwed the remains of the tissue into a ball, looked around for somewhere to put it, opened her handbag and dropped it inside.

'Which book did the chain in question come from?'

Angela blinked. 'I've no idea. Does it matter? Giles was a historian, so I expect the book was part of his research.'

'I bet Chief Inspector Arnold will be holding a press conference,' Libby murmured. 'Nothing he likes more than seeing his name in the papers and his face on the screen, and the national press will love this story. In fact, it's probably on the internet already.' Libby fell silent but her pulse raced. Another suspicious death in Somerset!

'There's more.' Angela fiddled with the strap of her bag.

'Go on.'

'They found something else. An object at – at the scene.'

'Come again?'

'A knitted scarf.'

Libby puffed air through her lips. 'Anything special about it?'

Angela's gaze faltered. She avoided Libby's face and focused on her own clenched hands, where the knuckles gleamed white. At last, she took a shaky breath and whispered, 'Hand-knitted in orange wool.'

Libby opened her mouth but closed it again. Was a hand-knitted scarf significant? It was winter after all. Everyone wore scarves and hats. On the other hand, how often did a man willingly wear a hand-knitted garment, especially a bright orange one? Most males never learned to knit, though a few did, of course. Fishermen; they were famous for it. And hadn't one Archbishop of Canterbury knitted jumpers? Still, he was the exception, rather than the rule. Most men wore hand-knitting only when the garment was made by a wife, girlfriend, or mother. In other words, a present, and one they felt duty bound to use.

Angela's reaction struck Libby as odd. Still pale and distressed, she seemed suddenly embarrassed. Could it be that Giles Temple's scarf was not a present from his wife? If her suspicion was right, it suggested a whole area of enquiry.

'Come on,' Libby said, keeping her tone gentle, for Angela was still pale and distressed. 'You can tell me. You know something about this scarf, don't you? Where did it come from?'

Angela looked Libby in the eye, suddenly defiant. 'We've been making scarves at the Knitters' Guild. Scarves, hats and gloves, but mostly, knitted squares. We're planning to yarnbomb Wells, but it's a secret. We don't want everyone in town to know about it. It would spoil the surprise.'

'Yarnbombing? What on earth...' Libby tapped a finger against her teeth, struggling to recall an article she'd read. 'Yarnbombing. Wait. Don't tell me. I know I've heard of it.' Angela managed a weak smile while Libby pondered.

The penny dropped. 'Got it.' Libby said. 'You drape lampposts and trees with knitted things.'

'Brightly coloured knitting, yes. It's supposed to cheer everyone up, so we thought this was a good time of year to try it, before spring arrives. Folk feel miserable in February, and it feels as though it will never be warm again.

'And the Wells event is also meant to celebrate the completion of renovations at the cathedral.' Scaffolding had obscured the West Front of Wells Cathedral for many months.

'Had Giles Temple heard about your plans?'

'Oh, yes; as have most of the staff at the cathedral, but they've been sworn to secrecy. Even the Dean's given it his blessing. Orange is one of the main colours we're using because it's bright.'

'It's not the only explanation,' Libby murmured, thinking aloud, 'but quite possibly, someone in the Guild knows Giles well and knitted a scarf for him.' She shot a sharp look at Angela, but her friend made no reply.

* * *

Angela, restored to calm, pronounced herself ready to leave the café, so the two friends and Bear clattered downstairs, the dog panting and waving his tail, already scenting exciting smells from the outside world.

Too late, Libby spotted a pile of books making its way up the stairs, apparently under its own steam. She tugged on the dog's lead. Bear skidded to a halt, but the man underneath the books panicked, tried to back away, lost his footing and grabbed at the handrail. The stack of books, magazines and documents exploded from his flailing arms and rocketed high in the air.

Libby watched, knuckles jammed against her mouth, as leather covered books thudded on the floor. A storm of loose papers followed, fluttering in ghastly slow motion to blanket the flagstones. Bear barked, delighted by the new game.

Angela shrieked. 'Dr Phillips, I'm so sorry...' She bent to retrieve a book, smoothing its Moroccan leather spine. Libby, mortified, shot a look at Bear that sent the animal's tail between his legs, and stooped to help.

'My books, my books,' the man stammered, breathlessly. 'What a day. Oh, my goodness me, what a terrible day.'

Angela examined the one in her hands. 'I don't think this one's damaged.'

The man stopped collecting paper long enough to glare at Libby through pebble spectacles. 'That dog of yours...'

'I know.' She was contrite. 'I'm sorry. He's a bit excited...' She stopped talking. Really, there was no excuse.

Angela intervened. 'Libby, this is Dr Phillips, the librarian.'

Libby, far too flustered to listen properly, barely registered the words.

'We won't shake hands.' Dr Phillips drew bushy brows together, raising himself to his full height, the shiny top of a bald head barely reaching Libby's shoulder.

'I'm so very sorry,' Libby stammered. Bear wagged an enthusiastic tail, trying to attract this new friend's attention.

'Just move that animal out of the way and let me pass.'

The significance of the pile of books and Angela's introduction finally filtered into Libby's brain. 'You're the librarian?' One of the first people Libby would want to talk to, for Giles had died in Dr Phillips' domain.

'Of course. Who might you be? Wait...' He juggled books and pointed with a bony finger. 'I recognise that dog. Biggest in Somerset, I bet. It belongs to Max Ramshore, doesn't it? That makes you Mrs Forest, the lady who solves mysteries.'

'Call me Libby.'

He ignored that. 'Today is a very bad day.' His wagged a gloomy head. 'We've had a serious incident.'

'The verger told us about it.'

'It's a most dreadful business. Nothing like it has ever happened before. You can't go inside, you know. The police have removed the – er – body, but access to the cathedral is strictly limited. The whole area's smothered in 'Crime Scene Do Not Enter' tape. No doubt I'll find fingerprint chemicals on the books and they'll all be ruined.' The librarian's face crinkled with worry.

Bear, disappointed to find this new friend refused to play, whined and stared hopefully at the exit. Libby ignored him, keeping a tight hold on the lead. 'You found the body, I think, Dr Phillips?'

He nodded. 'Lying on the floor, he was. Face all purple, tongue hanging out. Oh, my, that tongue. What a sight...'

Libby shook her head to rid it of the image. 'Could it be an accident?'

The librarian pursed his lips. 'Planning to investigate, are you? Good idea. The police spend too much time giving out speeding tickets these days. It could be months before they find the murderer. You get on to it; speed things up, Mrs Forest, so we can get back to normal.'

He balanced books on the stair rail, scratching his head with one hand. 'Now, what did you ask? Oh, yes, was it an accident? Hmm. Funny sort of accident, strangled by a chain round the neck.' He chortled. 'Someone did him in, and that's a fact.'

'What about suicide?'

'You mean, could he have made a noose from the chain and hung himself?' The librarian's face wrinkled in thought. 'No, that wouldn't work. The ceiling's too high. He wouldn't be able to get up there, even if he climbed on the benches...'

'Was the chain attached to anything?'

'No. Just round his neck.' The man seemed to warm to his topic. 'I'll tell you a funny thing.'

'Yes?'

'The knitted scarf was wrapped round on top of the chain. Strange. D'you see? On top of the chain, not underneath.' He pursed his lips. 'Couldn't kill himself first, then wrap a scarf round his neck, could he?'

His expression brightened. 'At least there wasn't any blood. Don't want blood on that old oak floor; seventeenth century, you know. You'd never get the stain out...'

3

GILES TEMPLE

Libby brought Angela back to the cottage she shared with her apprentice, Mandy, and Fuzzy the marmalade cat. She couldn't leave her friend alone to brood.

They settled in the living room of Hope Cottage with Bear guarding the door. Until recently, the room had been functional and reasonably comfortable, but unexciting. Libby's priority had been her state-of-the-art kitchen, where she'd developed recipes and written the book that kick-started her new career in Exham on Sea.

At Christmas, her son had presented her with a book of Danish style called 'Hygge.' The idea of warmth, cosiness and a happy atmosphere had captivated Libby. She'd bought cushions and a fluffy rug, positioned candles in the empty fireplace and brought in stools made from tree trunks. She'd even considered investing in a solid fuel heater.

Bear approved of the changes and spent as much time as possible stretched across the rug, snoring. Even Fuzzy deigned to curl up on the soft, fleece cushions.

Perhaps the atmosphere would help Angela relax and speak

freely. Since leaving the cathedral café, she'd been unusually quiet. Even now, she remained tense, gripping the arm of the sofa with rigid fingers and biting her lips.

Libby brought hot chocolate. Angela gave a wan smile and ran a finger round the rim of her mug. 'It's been such a shock. You don't expect people you know to die like that – in a library, of all places.'

'That's true.' Libby tried to sound non-committal. *I'm not getting involved. Not this time. I'm too busy with Robert's wedding and my business, and everything else...*

She'd been setting up a private investigation service with Max Ramshore, who currently worked for one of the more secretive branches of government on financial business, but recently, she'd suffered an attack of second thoughts. Not long ago, she'd been a recently widowed newcomer in Exham, building a small but successful business. She hadn't wanted a relationship with Max or anyone else. They'd worked together on a couple of mysterious murder cases and she'd discovered Max's skills fitted well with her own.

Besides that, the man was undeniably attractive, with bright blue eyes, a sharp intellect and a huge fund of common sense. Somehow, their agreement to work together had led to a closer personal relationship.

She wondered if Max was expecting them to become an item – even to get married, and she was scared. Things were moving too fast.

Whenever Libby thought about Max her heart fluttered, but her head throbbed with questions. Would they tire of one another if they worked too closely together? Would a successful partnership mean she had to walk away from the cakes and chocolate business she'd struggled so hard to establish, just as it was taking off? What about Mandy? Libby couldn't let her apprentice down.

She needed a breathing space, with time to think and no crime investigations, while Max finished his current assignment. Any inquiry into this most recent suspicious death was best left to the police.

Nevertheless, Libby's curiosity continued to nag, insistent as an itch. Asking a few questions wouldn't commit her to anything. It wasn't real investigating, was it? Besides, judging from the way Angela gulped hot chocolate, she was deeply stressed and clearly needed to talk.

Libby gave in to the temptation to find out more. 'Why was Giles in Wells? Does he have a family?'

'His home's in Birmingham. He's – I mean, he was – married, with two children. They're grown up, now. He's been coming to Wells for a couple of days every week, working late into the night and travelling home as often as possible.' Angela shot a glance at Libby. 'He's nothing to do with Wells Cathedral. He's a history lecturer, studying texts from the sixteenth century and writing a book about old beliefs and superstitions...'

Her voice tailed away, but Libby hardly noticed. She'd stopped listening. The thought of Giles Temple's wife had sent a shiver down her spine. The police, probably on the way to Birmingham right now, would have to break the news to Mrs Temple. Libby pictured a cheerful woman opening a neat front door, her smile freezing on her face as the officer asked permission to come inside.

How quickly would realisation dawn? When would Mrs Temple understand she'd become a widow? Her husband had gone forever. He would not return home for dinner, that day or any other. She'd have to tell their children.

What would she do? Collapse on the floor, scream and shout,

or hide her feelings with a clenched jaw and stiff upper lip until the police left and she could grieve in peace?

Libby blinked and forced her focus back to her friend. 'Giles was a lovely man,' Angela was saying. 'Gentle and kind. I can't imagine why anyone would want to kill him in such a horrid way; and in the cathedral, too.'

'It's certainly novel,' Libby mused. 'Strangled with a chain. That's a nasty way to go.'

Angela fingered the pearls in her necklace. 'Then, there's the scarf.'

'Now, that's interesting. I wish I could see it. I suppose Giles Temple wasn't a member of the Knitters' Guild?'

Her friend spluttered. 'Not likely. He was too old school. You know, women cook and knit, men work and think.' Angela's hand flew to her mouth. 'Oh dear, that doesn't sound kind at all. I don't mean he was a bully. I'm sure he couldn't have been. He was much too gentle.'

Her eyes met Libby's in a moment of shared understanding. Both had endured bullying husbands who liked to keep a wife in her place. A guilty-twinge reminded Libby she'd felt nothing but relief when Trevor, her own husband, died. But then, he'd been secretly money-laundering, so Libby had no need to feel guilty. Unfortunately, the habit died hard.

Angela pulled out her phone. 'How silly of me. I can show you a photo of Giles, taken in the library during a tour.' She flicked through screens on her phone, using a forefinger to swipe awkwardly from one picture to another. 'Here it is.'

She angled the phone towards Libby and the picture disappeared. Angela clicked her tongue. 'I'll never get used to this phone.'

Libby laughed, glad of the break in tension. 'Mandy never goes anywhere without her mobile, but I can't get the hang of mine at all. I think you have to be young – preferably under thirty-five.' She crossed the room to sit on the sofa beside Angela, peering over her friend's shoulder as the picture returned.

Libby took in the details; rows of heavy, leather-bound books, neatly arranged on wooden shelves, their heavy chains dangling. Nearby, a small group of visitors peered into a glass display case. The camera had caught Giles Temple, one of two men in the group, with his mouth open. His hair was sparse, a rim of grey-speckled brown tufts worn a shade too long for Libby's taste. Round, tortoiseshell glasses hooked onto a pair of over-large ears.

'I'm afraid I took him by surprise,' Angela murmured.

'Who are the other people? Oh, that's the librarian.'

Angela pointed. 'The lady in the middle of the picture, next to Giles, is the Dean's wife, Amelia Weir. She works in the library once a week, as I do, but on different days. I don't know her well.'

Mrs Weir, much younger than Libby or Angela, stood very close to Giles Temple. Angela's voice had been sharp. Libby shot a glance at her face. Two angry furrows had appeared on her forehead. Could Amelia Weir and Angela both have had a soft spot for this Giles?

For now, Libby changed the subject. 'I think I need to know more about the Guild's yarnbombing.'

'There's a session this evening. Why don't you come along and meet the members?'

'I'll be there. I can't knit, but I'll bring cake.'

4

KNITTERS' GUILD

'What should I wear to a Knitters' Guild meeting?' Libby asked Bear. 'A knitted jumper's required, I suppose. Anyway, it's bound to be cold.' She'd been to history society meetings in the area before and learned to take warm clothes.

The dog gazed into her face; his eyes mournful. Libby frowned. 'Stop looking at me like that. You can't come.'

Three sweaters lay on the bed. The Arran cable tempted her, for the evening was chilly, but it made Libby look fat. 'I've been sampling too many chocolates, Bear. Time to take myself in hand. Tomorrow, maybe.'

She put the sweater back in the drawer. Fast losing patience, she grabbed a cheerful red and yellow striped jersey and shrugged it over her head. 'Will they know I didn't knit it myself?'

Bear lay on his back, inviting Libby to scratch his stomach, hoping to dissuade her from leaving him. 'Oh, very well. You can come as my guard dog. Just behave yourself and don't deposit dog hair all over the knitting.' Bear clattered towards the front door. Fuzzy the cat watched, envy glittering in her green eyes.

Fuzzy adored Bear. 'Sorry, you can't come with us, Fuzz, but

I've left the door of the airing cupboard open. It's as warm as toast.' The airing cupboard was one of Fuzzy's cherished spots.

Libby emptied a can of the best wild red salmon into the cat's dish. Fuzzy pretended not to notice, but as soon as Libby closed the door, she'd gobble every scrap. Libby pulled on a woolly hat. 'Come on, Bear. Let's go.'

She felt a twinge of guilt. She spent so much time with Bear and Fuzzy these days that she'd given little thought to the dog she'd taken under her wing when she first arrived in Exham on Sea.

She'd been walking with Shipley, a friendly, excitable springer spaniel, when she came across a dead rock singer under Exham's unique, wooden legged lighthouse.

That encounter had begun her adventures in crime solving.

Poor Shipley had been abandoned when his owner, Marina, left the area, and currently lived with the vet. Maybe Libby could offer to walk him from time to time, as she used to.

Not tonight, though. The thought of the energetic Shipley at a Knitters' Guild meeting made her shudder. The wool would be chewed to pieces or tied in knots in no time.

The street was dark tonight. To make financial savings and reduce light pollution, Exham's town council had dimmed the streetlamps. As a result, stars glittered across a clear sky. The moon hung low, a shimmering crescent in crisp air. Libby inhaled the unmistakable scent of the ocean. The beach lay out of sight of her cottage, but it filled the air with the sharp smell of ozone.

She brushed gloved hands through a rosemary bush outside and inhaled. Few plants survived the salty winds that speckled and corroded every shiny brass number on Libby's front door, but rosemary and lavender flourished. They were her favourite herbs. She remembered a recipe she'd been developing; tea bread flavoured with rosemary. She'd planned to work on it tonight, but she was too intrigued by the Knitters' Guild to stay at home. Tea loaves could wait.

She shivered and loaded Bear into her purple Citroen, the car so small he overflowed across the whole back seat. If she hadn't quarrelled with Max before his current trip to London, she'd have borrowed the Land Rover.

They'd been arguing for weeks over silly things like Bear's tendency to dig up Libby's lawn, or whether Libby was unreasonable to beg her daughter to return home from her working holiday in South America for Christmas. Max advised leaving well alone, for Ali would come home when she was ready, but Libby wanted her family together. In the end, Robert and Sarah had stayed at Hope Cottage, Max had dropped in on Christmas Day and Libby had spent a tearful half-hour on the phone to Ali.

Max had been away for a few days, now, and Libby could see with clearer eyes. She suspected they were finding excuses for keeping their distance from each other, because both had endured unsuccessful marriages in the past.

Thinking of Max today, an ache of longing caught Libby by surprise. She missed him.

Determined not to be needy, she drove on through the darkness, meeting few other cars on such a chilly winter night. Anyone with good sense was at home, warm and cosy.

As she braked outside the tiny village hall where the knitters gathered, the door flew open and light, laughter and coffee smells spilled out.

Angela led her inside. 'Look, everyone, Libby's brought treats.'

'You'll soon get used to us,' bellowed a big-boned, hearty woman with a beaky nose, as she tucked into a slice of Dundee cake. Her voice boomed, deep and mannish. A single streak of bright green ran through a shock of wild grey hair. 'I'm June. Like the song: busting out all over.' She cackled.

Libby settled Bear in a corner with a huge chew, knowing he'd finish it in less than half an hour. The room was small and faintly oppressive. An electric fire hung awkwardly from the ceiling, throwing heat on the top of Libby's head while her feet remained chilled. 'How does this yarnbombing work, exactly?'

June hooted. 'It's art, you know. At any rate, it's a grand excuse to creep out in the middle of the night and tie things to lamp posts without being arrested. That's the truth of it. The fun starts the next day when folk see what we've done. Can't wait to see their faces. Tried it in Trivington a year ago. Just what Wells needs to liven it up.'

'Not that it needs livening up, of course.' Angela was always alert in case someone should be offended.

'Manner of speech, that's all. Livvy'll soon get used to me.'

'It's Libby, actually.'

June roared with laughter.

A plump, motherly woman poured tea from an old brown teapot. 'I don't do the bombing for fun, you know. I knit useful things, like hats and scarves. I'm Ruby, by the way. I shall hang my work on benches and people who need them can take them home. It helps the less fortunate. I call it 'giving back to society.''

Another voice intervened. 'Do you remember that time we hung knitted underwear from the tower on Glastonbury Tor? The National Trust people were furious.'

Ruby glared but the other woman ignored her. Tiny and thin, she radiated energy. 'I'm Vera, by the way. Welcome to our group. You knit, of course?'

'I'm afraid not. Well, my mother taught me when I was small, but I haven't knitted for years.'

June swooped, green hair awry. 'Now's your chance to take it up again, then. Size ten needles and double knitting wool. That'll do the trick. You'll finish a square in no time.'

Plied with balls of every colour, Libby avoided orange and yellow, choosing instead the quietest colour available, royal blue. She settled on a wooden chair and allowed the plump mother figure, Ruby, to elbow June aside, cast on a row of stitches and hand them over.

Struggling with wool that stuck to her unpractised, fumbling fingers, Libby listened as the women talked. Silently, she repeated her vow not to investigate, although the knitters' unguarded thoughts would be fascinating. They were all connected with the cathedral, as volunteers, worshippers or friends of the clergy. As they chattered, needles flashed and balls of wool turned, like magic, into socks, scarves and hats.

News of the murder had spread like wildfire and everyone had a theory. June ran both hands through her hair until the green stripe stood on end, like an exotic parrot perched on top of her head. 'I reckon the Dean did it. Never liked the man. Always after money. Funds for clock renovation, contributions for new vestments. Can't say good morning without begging.'

'Poor man, it's his job, you know,' Angela soothed. 'He was very kind to me when my husband died.'

June grunted, bit the end off a strand of wool, threw a yellow square onto the table and cast on a fresh row of orange stitches.

Vera giggled. 'I don't want to speak ill of the dead, but that Mr Temple was a right one for the ladies.'

Libby felt Angela stiffen. 'How do you mean?' she asked, keeping her voice neutral.

Vera glanced round, nostrils flared, checking all eyes were on her. 'I saw him in The Swan with the Dean's wife.' She stopped knitting and hissed, in a loud stage whisper, 'I wouldn't be surprised if the Dean did it. You know—a crime of passion.'

5

CHIEF INSPECTOR ARNOLD

A stunned silence followed Vera's remark. Libby waited to see who'd speak first, shooting a surreptitious glance round her companions to judge their reactions. Angela's face turned puce red, her lips pressed tightly together. June's eyes bulged. *A frog. That's what she looks like. A great green frog.* Ruby poured tea. 'I think it's rather unkind to jump to conclusions. I've always had the greatest respect for our Dean. You should be ashamed of yourself, Vera.'

Vera shrugged, not the least bit ashamed. 'I speak as I find.'

'What exactly is that supposed to mean, Vera?' Angela's voice was sharp enough to slice a finger. Libby, eyes on her knitting, concealed a grin.

'I mean,' said Vera, 'that I can follow evidence just as well as our new, so-called member, here.' Scorn dripped from the words. 'Isn't it true you're a kind of amateur sleuth, Mrs Forest, and you're here to find out if one of us had anything to do with the murder?'

'What if she is?' Angela's eyes flashed. Libby thought she'd never seen her so furious. 'Libby has a wonderful track record of solving mysteries.'

'Well, she makes a good cake, I'd say that for her,' observed June, tucking in to a second slice. 'If she can find the killer, good on her, that's what I say.'

Libby put aside her square of dropped stitches, the wool grey from over-handling. 'You're quite right. I've been involved in other cases and I've had some luck, but I don't know the Dean or Mr Temple, or anyone else at the cathedral except Angela, and I'm not investigating. I trust the police.' She hesitated, exchanged a glance with Angela and decided not to mention the orange scarf.

Vera's eyes were wide. 'What if there's another murder. Is it likely, do you think?'

Libby shrugged. 'It happens. It depends on why Giles Temple was murdered, and who killed him.'

The motherly Ruby brushed crumbs from her bosom. 'In that case, we must find the murderer as soon as possible. I agree with June. I, for one, never liked that Dr Weir, the Dean. He's been here three years, and what's he done for the cathedral? Included a lot of silly new services for a bunch of noisy children, that's what.'

June wiped her mouth. 'Sooner they find the killer, the better. Come on, Vera, tell us a bit more. You saw Giles Temple meeting the Dean's wife. Were they having an affair?'

Vera hesitated, perhaps thinking better of her accusations. 'Dr Weir's wife is a historian. So was Giles Temple. I suppose they might have been comparing notes.' Bouncing back, she finished, 'But they seemed pretty friendly, if you ask me.'

A question was on the tip of Libby's tongue, but before she could speak someone hammered on the door. Vera jumped, tea slopping from her cup as the door swung open. Libby recognised Chief Inspector Arnold and her heart sank. He made no secret of the fact he thought Libby a nuisance, even when she helped untangle a case. He'd been furious when she outdid the police and solved the murder at the lighthouse.

Uniform buttons glinting, he stepped inside and took a long, slow look round the room, enjoying the moment. His close-set eyes glittered. 'Sorry to disturb you, ladies.' The high-pitched voice grated on Libby's ears. 'I need a word with you. I expect you've heard about the incident at the cathedral.'

His gaze fell on Libby. 'Well, well.' He fingered his chin. 'Fancy meeting you here, Mrs Forest. Often turn up, don't you, when there's a crime? I'll be suspecting you're behind the murder, if you're not careful. Ha,ha.' The laugh was unconvincing, the small black eyes sharp. 'Trying to get one over on the police, I suppose.'

'Are we all suspects?' giggled Vera. 'How exciting.'

The chief inspector smiled through tight lips. 'There'll be time for that, later. We're just making preliminary inquiries at the moment. It's normal police procedure, nothing to be concerned about. I believe you all knew the deceased, Mr Giles Temple.' Heads nodded. 'What about you, Mrs Forest? Was he one of your acquaintances?'

Libby shook her head. 'I never met him.'

'And are you a member of the Knitters' Guild? I can't seem to find your name anywhere on this list.' He ran a long finger down a sheet of paper, his lips twitching. 'Or maybe you work in the cathedral?'

Libby tried not to squirm under the sarcasm. 'No, I was just...' She stopped.

'Quite. I suggest you get back to your chocolates and leave the police work to the professionals.' Libby turned to gather up the empty cake tin and call Bear to her side. The chief inspector used a finger and thumb to pick up the ragged, unfinished square she'd been working on. 'Not a professional knitter, I see.'

6

MAX

Libby curled her feet on the sofa and chewed a fingernail. Max had rung as arranged, soon after she arrived home, but their conversation had been difficult and unsatisfactory.

'I've cut down my consultancy work,' he reminded her, 'so at least one of us is committed to the future. Time to make your mind up, Libby. Are we a partnership, or not?'

'Don't hassle me. I need to think.'

'I don't know why you've suddenly developed cold feet. You usually jump headfirst into everything. once or twice you've almost got yourself killed as a result. No one could call you timid, so why are you being indecisive, now? Am I scary?'

A lump formed in Libby's throat. 'You're not at all scary, Max. Try to understand. I'm not only grappling with the implications of a private investigation business on my cakes and chocolates, although that's complicated enough. There's the other thing, too.'

'Us, you mean? Look we've talked about the future, and we're not in a hurry. It's not as though we're getting married.'

'No, but what are we doing. I mean, if we did, where would we live? In your house? If we did that, what about my cottage? I can't just sell it. It's important to me and besides, I run the chocolate business from the kitchen. You see what I mean?'

Max sighed. 'It's not complicated at all. You're trying to think of problems. Be honest with me, Libby. We're partners, aren't we? We do well together. Why don't we take things further? Be real partners, not just in business?'

She gulped. What did Max really want? Was he proposing marriage? Out of the blue, like this? 'That's not fair. Not on the phone.'

There was a long silence. 'Max? Are you still there?' Libby's voice sounded very small.

'OK. I won't pin you down over the phone. Not about getting married, anyway. I suppose that's not fair.'

'Not very romantic,' she mumbled.

His laugh sounded rueful. 'No, I suppose not, but being away from you made me think.'

He cleared his throat. 'We don't need to commit. Not yet. But I won't wait for ever. When I get home in a couple of days, I'm going to set up the business. You can join me, or not. Up to you.'

Libby swallowed but the lump remained. 'Let's talk about it when you come home.'

'Meanwhile,' Max dropped the serious tone. 'Tell me about this murder you're determined not to investigate.'

Relieved to change the subject, Libby told him about the cathedral library and the orange scarf, her spirits lifting as he laughed at her description of the knitters. 'Angela's upset. She says this Giles Temple was just a friend, but I don't think she's telling me the whole truth.'

'And the police? Is Joe part of the inquiry?' Max's son, a detective sergeant, had worked on several other murder investigations.

'I haven't spoken to him. Chief Inspector Arnold appeared at the Knitters' Guild, though, and sent me home. I could have slapped his smug face.'

'Turn the other cheek. You should hear the abuse I had from the company I visited today, when I questioned their shady accounts. Don't let Arnold intimidate you.'

'I won't. Anyway, I won't see him again. I'm not investigating, remember?'

'You should at least go back to another meeting. It's time you added knitting to your talents, and I could use a new sweater.'

Libby giggled. 'You can knit your own.'

'Did you discover any other keen knitters? Those who didn't attend the meeting.'

'Yes, Angela dropped a list of names through the letter box on her way home. They're planning a surprise for Wells, you see. A yarnbombing.'

Max chuckled. 'OK. I give up. What's a yarnbomb?'

Libby recited the details. 'It's due next week, on Tuesday, at dead of night.'

'Tuesday. Good, I'll be back by then. I wouldn't miss it for the world. By the way, some old colleagues have agreed to send some investigative work my way. That would give our business a boost.'

Max went on, 'And everyone in Somerset must have heard about Libby Forest, female sleuth, by now.'

'OK, you know I'm tempted to work with you, Max. Leave it for now. I don't want to give up my own business. Not yet, anyway.'

'You don't have to. Just cut back a little. Give Mandy more to do and take on another assistant. Forget the cakes and stick with the chocolates.'

'I'll think about it.' Libby giggled.

'What is it?'

'I just realised the truth. You can't live without my chocolates.'

'Ah. You found me out.' His voice softened. 'I'm looking forward to coming home. Things will work out, you know. Oh, by the way, I'm bringing a colleague. An American.'

'Anyone I know?'

'No, but you'll love him, though not too much, I hope. He's younger than me.'

'I like the sound of him already. What's the occasion?'

'Some work he's doing.' Max's voice was vague. 'I thought I'd ask a few people round to meet him. His name's Reg Talbot, by the way. I thought, Robert and Sarah. You said they were planning to visit, to stay with her parents while they make wedding plans, read the banns and so forth. Mandy and Steve, of course.'

Libby took a deep breath. She'd mentioned Max to her son, Robert, but they hadn't met. This could be tricky. 'I don't know about Steve. He and Mandy had a falling out, and I'm not sure they're still an item. I'll check.'

'Cheer up. It'll be fun.' Libby's phone buzzed.

She had a text, from Angela.

I have to see you. Right now.

* * *

Angela had sounded desperate. The Citroen hurtled towards her house, squealing round corners as dread squeezed Libby's insides. Angela would only send such a message in dire circumstances.

She must have been watching from a window, for the door was already open when Libby ran up the path. 'What's the matter?'

'I'm so glad you're here. I don't know what to do.'

'Sit down, collect your thoughts and explain.'

Angela paced round her elegant, grey-painted room, moving expensive scented candles and straightening books in an already tidy bookcase. 'There's something I kept from you. I hoped it didn't matter, but it's been eating away at me.'

Libby thought for a moment, reviewing their conversation in the café. 'I had a feeling you weren't being entirely honest. It's the scarf, isn't it?' Her friend rubbed invisible specks of dirt from an over-mantle mirror, avoiding Libby's eyes. 'Did you give it to Giles Temple?'

Angela grabbed a tissue from a nearby box. 'It was a joke, just between the two of us. We laughed about the yarnbombing. You know, how tacky and bright it was going to be. Giles said no one would ever wear anything in those colours. Well, I couldn't resist knitting the brightest scarf I could and giving it to Giles. He promised to wear it. It was just a joke.' She dabbed at her eyes. 'What will the police think?'

Libby's brain clicked into gear. The presence of the scarf at the murder scene made Angela a prime suspect. She knew Giles was a married man, and she'd given him a gift she made herself. It looked suspicious, and Libby was sure, now, that the two of them had grown close. Libby groaned. She knew what was coming.

Angela said, 'Please, help me, Libby. I'm scared. You see, if the police know I spent a lot of time with Giles—' She winced, 'with him being married, they might think I had something to do with it. Revenge, if he was throwing me over, or something like that.'

Her cheeks glowed bright red. 'Find out who killed Giles. That's the only way I'll feel safe. You can't just leave it to the police. Everyone knows they're over-stretched. They'll find out about the scarf, decide I killed him and won't look for anyone else.'

Libby's head drooped as her hopes of a quiet life, with time to make decisions about the future, evaporated. Angela, normally so calm, looked terrified. Smudges of mascara ran into tiny lines around her eyes.

Libby rose and offered another tissue. 'I'll try to help, on one condition.'

'Anything.' Angela's face lit up. 'Anything at all.'

Libby hid a wry smile. Angela wasn't going to like her next words, but that was too bad. 'I can't help unless you swear you had nothing to do with Giles Temple's death.'

A flush covered Angela's face from neck to hairline. For a second, her eyes flashed anger. Slowly, she gained control. When she spoke, her voice grated, harsh and strained. 'I understand why you have to ask, Libby. I suppose you need to be sure. On my honour, I swear I didn't kill Giles Temple and I don't know who did.'

7

BAKERY

Libby spent the next morning with Mandy, working at the bakery. In the shop, she had no spare time to think of Max, or worry about Angela, or Giles Temple's murder. Mandy was unusually quiet. Libby supposed she was brooding about the quarrel with Steve.

Frank, the baker, had converted half the shop to a display space for chocolates, and his girth was expanding as a result. 'The wife's sending me out running every evening.' He heaved a sigh. 'I can resist bread and cakes, all except your squishy chocolate log...'

He centred a slice on a plate. 'But those chocs'll be the death of me. Still,' his long face lightened. 'My daily shuffle gets me out of the house for a bit of peace.'

He finished the last morsel and wiped his mouth. 'Delicious. Ah well. No peace for the wicked. They'll be coming in for their lunch time sandwiches, any minute now, wanting to talk about this affair over at the cathedral. I'll be off.'

Frank, unique in Exham on Sea, hated gossip. Mandy once

suggested he'd been bullied in childhood. 'Impossible. He's six feet tall with shoulders like bill-boards,' Libby objected.

'Maybe he grew after leaving school.' Frank made himself scarce whenever the door opened, leaving Libby, Mandy or one of his new part-timers in charge.

Along with bread, cakes and chocolates, the shop functioned as a branch of the local Exham grapevine, and sure enough, the shop soon buzzed with theories about the murder in the cathedral.

'I made a delivery there, just the day before he was found.' Gladys, the owner of the flower shop, panted with excitement. 'Imagine, it could have been me, lying dead on the floor.'

'Never been caught in a library, though, have you,' jeered one of the paper boys, paying for a pair of Belgian buns with a crumpled note, 'Have to be able to read.'

'I hope you won't be eating both those buns for your lunch,' Mandy snapped. 'All that sugar – you won't be able to walk. And don't lean your bike against the window. There's a sign there, you know. Maybe it's you who can't read.'

Libby shot a glance at Mandy. She was cranky today.

Gladys handed over a twenty pound note in payment for a waist-watching salad and glowered at the boy as she waited for change. 'Getting back to the cathedral. I was talking to the Bishop's wife, the other day. You know, the Bishop of Bath and Wells.'

She peeped under her lashes at the queue of customers, checking that they were listening and were suitably impressed. 'She told me the man who died, Giles something, was researching old stories from the past, about ghosts and the supernatural and such like. She said it wasn't a very suitable subject for a cathedral library, and I for one, agree.'

'Maybe it was a ghost that did him in,' suggested a young man. New to Libby, he wore the estate agent uniform of short gelled hair, shiny pointed shoes and a vivid pink shirt. Exham was full of estate agents. House prices were rumoured to be due to rocket, now a new nuclear power station was being built nearby, at Hinckley Point.

The doorbell chimed and local solicitor, Samantha Watson, entered. Samantha, who was engaged to be married to the pompous Chief Inspector Arnold, disliked Libby as an interfering newcomer to Exham and only graced the bakery with her presence when she had a spicy police titbit to share.

'Pillow talk from her fiancé,' Max called it. Libby waited, expectant. Samantha's tips had been useful in the past, though Libby would die rather than admit it. The solicitor already thought far too well of herself.

She inspected Mandy from head to toe. 'What an original necklace, dear, and on such a heavy chain. A Celtic cross, isn't it? Did you know, the murderer used a chain to kill his victim in the cathedral library?'

Mandy rose to the bait before Libby could intervene. 'We did, as it happens.'

'Chief Inspector Arnold told me the chain was made of forged steel. Incredibly strong. But, that's not all...'

'Go on,' said Gladys, as Samantha produced a dramatic pause.

'Well, I'm not sure I ought to tell you. Police business, you know. In fact, I think perhaps I should wait. There's going to be a press conference in half an hour. I'll just say this – don't miss it. You'll hear something very interesting if you watch the local news.'

The paper boy tore off a slab of bun and spoke with his mouth full. 'That Inspector—'

'Chief Inspector,' Samantha corrected.

The boy licked his lips. 'Whatever. He'd better not come after our Dan.'

'Dan who?'

'My brother, Dan. He was at school with those lads who had a cannabis farm, and he reckons the cops are out to get him.'

Samantha looked smug. 'Those boys were lucky. They were given suspended sentences. Maybe your Dan should have been in court with them.' She glanced sideways at Libby. 'I worked on the case, you know.'

The boy wiped his mouth on a grubby sleeve, elbowed the door, and cycled away. Gladys huffed. 'Rude, that boy, like all his family. Thinks the world owes him a living.'

Samantha turned back to Mandy. 'Anyway, dear, perhaps you should rethink your jewellery. You don't want to be a suspect in a murder case, do you? It wouldn't be easy to persuade the judge to let you off lightly.'

8

PRESS CONFERENCE

Mandy served the remaining customers in tight-lipped silence, clearly upset by Samantha's remarks. The final customer, Mr Ali from the Indian restaurant, took an impossibly long time to choose a roll, settling at last on salmon and cucumber. A round, jovial man, he'd once confided in Libby how much he hated the 'English curry' his customers demanded. 'I wish I could serve some of the food my mother used to make, but it wouldn't go down well. Not enough spice, too many vegetables,' he'd sighed.

'Mrs Watson practically accused me.' Mandy burst out as the door closed.

'It's not you. She just likes winding people up,' Libby soothed. 'Ignore her.'

'Easy for you to say,' Mandy muttered, just loud enough for Libby to hear.

Better to ignore that. Mandy would cool down soon enough. Libby switched on the television in the back of the bakery as Frank returned. 'The press conference is about to start.'

Sure enough, Chief Inspector Arnold sat behind a long table,

flanked by a female police constable on one side and Detective
Sergeant Joe Ramshore, Max's son, on the other.

The police constable introduced Arnold, who nodded at the
assembled body of local and national press. Arnold's face was
composed, schooled into an ostentatious, solemn expression.

'Good afternoon, ladies and gentlemen. Thank you for
attending on such short notice. I called this press conference to
discuss the suspicious death of a man in the library of Wells
Cathedral. The first forty-eight hours after a murder are vital.' He
blinked as a press camera flashed. 'I expect anyone holding information that might help our inquiries to step forward.'

Mandy leaned closer to Libby. 'He can't help sounding up
himself, can he?'

Libby said, 'He's not my favourite person. How he loves to be
in front of the cameras.'

Glad to see some of her apprentice's good humour had
returned, she focused on the TV. Now she'd promised Angela
she'd make inquiries, she needed to know all the available facts.

Arnold performed well, she had to admit, with just the right
amount of gravitas. Libby was impressed against her will. No
wonder the man had risen so fast through the ranks. She pulled
out a pen and scribbled in her newest notebook. The time of the
victim's death had not been established, but the pathologist had
identified a window of six hours, from the time Mr Temple spoke
to the librarian at six o'clock in the evening, to midnight. Libby
wrote, *Rigor mortis?*

'Did anyone notice Mr Temple near the cathedral after six
o'clock?' the chief inspector asked. 'We're keen to speak to the last
person to see him.'

Mandy, scrubbing the counter, paused to chortle. 'That would
be the killer, then. He was the last one to see the victim.'

'Shh. He's still talking.'

'The forensic pathologist suggests midnight is probably the latest possible time for the crime to have been committed. Anyone in the cathedral or the streets nearby, should come forward. We want to know if anyone entered the building or behaved suspiciously.'

The chief inspector spoke directly to the camera. 'Were you in Wells that night? Did you see anything strange? The police are waiting for your call.'

Libby murmured, 'They'll be swamped with statements. How many children board at Wells Cathedral School? I bet some were in town, and they'll all have bright ideas.'

The chief inspector added details. 'The last service at the cathedral, Evensong, finished around six o'clock. There was no concert in the building that night.'

'Don't expect many folks attended evening service in the middle of the week,' Frank pointed out. 'Not in winter.'

The chief inspector invited the press to ask questions, letting Joe Ramshore answer. 'Typical,' said Mandy. 'Everything left to his team while he claims the credit.'

Frank laughed. 'He's the boss.'

A journalist raised a hand, waited for a microphone to arrive and asked, 'Are there any significant clues as to the identity of the criminal, Chief Inspector Arnold?'

Arnold beamed at the journalist's use of his full title. 'We have several lines of enquiry, all of which will be pursued with the utmost diligence. However, I would like to bring one item to your attention. This was found near the body.'

With a flourish, he waved an arm. Libby squinted at the screen as he held up Angela's orange scarf.

As cameras flashed and whirred, Arnold explained, 'This is a hand-knitted scarf. Mr Temple was not an *aficionado* of the art and craft of knitting.' Scorn oozed from his voice.

Mandy muttered, 'An *afici* – what?' Libby put a finger to her lips. She needed to hear every word.

'His wife does not recognise the scarf as belonging to herself or anyone she knows. She has never seen her late husband wear it. This item may be important, so we would like you to think carefully. Have you ever seen this scarf? If so, please make yourself known to the police.'

Joe gave the details of contact numbers for the incident room in Vicars Close, near the cathedral, and the press conference ended. Libby bit her lip. She must tell Joe of Angela's confession about her relationship with Giles Temple.

* * *

The phone rang before Libby could key in Joe's number. 'Hi, Mrs Forest? It's Joe here, Joe Ramshore.'

'That's a coincidence. I was about to ring you. By the way, Joe, I think it's time you called me Libby, like everyone else does. It can't be so hard, now you're talking to Max again.'

'Sorry. Libby. Look here, I can't speak for long. I'm just leaving the press conference.'

'I've been watching it.'

'Can I come over in the next day or so? There's something I want to run past you.'

'Well yes, of course. I need to speak to you, too. How about tomorrow morning, about nine?'

'Great, thanks. See you then.'

Libby frowned. 'That was weird. Joe wants to talk to me. I wonder what's happened.' There was a note of urgency in Joe's voice that unsettled Libby. Still, his visit would give her an opportunity to worm information out of him, once she'd shared Angela's confession.

Mandy polished the oven door until it sparkled. 'Don't forget you're taking me driving tonight.'

Libby stiffened. She'd forgotten that promise. Her heart sank, but she couldn't admit it. Not with Mandy in today's touchy mood.

Frank waved them away, 'It sounds like you two need to get off. I can manage the rest of the afternoon now the rush is over.'

Libby almost made it to the door before her phone rang again. 'Libby Forest here.'

'Oh, hello. You don't know me,' said a deep, plummy female voice with immaculate vowels, 'but I visited the vet today, and she recommended you.'

The vet? Libby thought hard, determined to remember the vet's name. 'Oh, yes, Tanya Ross. I know her.'

'She said you solve mysteries. I looked you up on the local news website and found you've been involved in a few little matters with some success, so I decided to give you a ring.'

She fell silent. Libby spoke cautiously, 'How can I help you?'

'It's my cat. He's disappeared into thin air. I'd like you to find him for me?'

'Your cat?'

Mandy's eyes were on stalks and Libby had to turn away to keep from bursting into laughter. 'I – er – I don't know.'

'I thought you were a private investigator,' the woman accused.

'No. Well – it's true I've inquired into a few things, but I've never dealt with lost animals. Except my own, of course...' Libby bit her tongue. Her first instinct was to refuse this case. She gave an exaggerated shrug and whispered to Mandy, 'What should I do?'

'Go for it, Mrs F.'

Perhaps unravelling a less stressful mystery might offer Libby perspective on the life of a private investigator. A lost cat couldn't be too difficult. Libby put on her best telephone voice and asserted herself. 'Maybe we should meet tomorrow.'

'Not until then?'

'I'm afraid not. Give me your details and I'll come at eleven. That's the earliest I can manage.'

'Oh, well, that's better than nothing, I suppose.' The woman gave her name.

'Marchant,' Libby repeated, making a note.

'Mrs.'

The call ended. Libby sighed. 'I must be crazy.'

Mandy leaned on the counter. 'I wonder why Joe wants to see you. I bet Chief Inspector Arnold won't listen to his ideas. By the way, while you were out yesterday, Jumbles sent us another big order. They need, like, twice as many chocolates as usual next week.'

Libby's legs wobbled and she sank onto a chair. 'This is impossible. There aren't enough hours in a day.'

'It's the price of success. Get used to it.'

'Is it? It feels exhausting. Will you visit Jumbles? Use all your charm and see how long they can give us.' The Jumbles account was the first one Mandy had negotiated alone.

She leaned over Libby's shoulder to read the address. 'Mrs Marchant. The Cedars. Wow, sounds posh. I bet you can charge her, like, a fortune. She must be rolling in dosh, and her cats are her babies. I think you've hit the big time.'

9

DRIVING LESSON

Mandy adjusted the driving seat in Libby's little purple Citroen and rattled the keys. Libby pulled her seatbelt tight. 'Tell me again, exactly how many lessons have you had?'

'Loads. The instructor said I need to practice, but I'm quite safe, honest.'

'Maybe I should drive us to the car park and start there...'

Mandy snorted, turned the key in the ignition and revved the engine. Libby shuddered as it howled. 'Oops. Sorry, Mrs F.'

She released the handbrake and the car lurched forward. 'Did you look behind?' Libby asked.

'Course. Nothing coming. Let's roll.'

The car moved sedately down the street, stopping neatly to turn at the T-junction, and Libby's clenched jaw began to relax. Mandy was perfectly competent. 'Were you trying to scare me, by any chance?'

Mandy giggled. 'Sorry, couldn't resist. Actually, my instructor's put me in for my test. It's in three weeks, but I need to practice parallel parking.'

Libby groaned. 'Definitely need to head for the car park, then, and I'm not sure I can help.'

'I know. You'd drive three times round town rather than reverse into a space.'

Half an hour later, Mandy had practiced the manoeuvre a dozen times. She drew to a halt facing the beach. 'Come on, then, out with it.'

Libby gulped, wrong footed. 'Out with what?'

'I saw you with Mrs Miles in the cathedral café when Steve and I quarrelled. I know you're dying to hear all about it. Why haven't you asked me?'

'I didn't want to interfere, but if you want to tell me about it, I'd like to help.' So, this was why Mandy suddenly needed driving practice; she wanted to talk. It was easier to share confidences in a car. Libby felt a warm glow. She valued Mandy's friendship.

'Well, we've split up. Steve keeps asking me to go to London at the weekend, but I don't see why I should.'

'Is it the expense?' Mandy's pay as an apprentice wasn't great, and the train to Paddington cost a fortune. 'You should be able to get a student discount, and...'

Mandy shook her head. 'It's not that. It's my clausta— thingy.'

Libby half turned in her seat. 'Your clausta— do you mean claustrophobia?'

Mandy nodded. 'I get it in the train. Or a coach.'

'And you haven't told Steve?'

'He'll think I'm pathetic. He wanted me to go to a concert and I said I would, but then I panicked and told him I was ill.'

'And he didn't believe you.'

'He thought I didn't want to go with him, and he took Alice, instead.'

'That's why you're suddenly so keen to take a driving test. You're planning to drive down to London?'

Mandy nodded. 'I'm fine in a car. I think it's all the other people on the train that cause the trouble. They seem so close, almost on top of me, so I can't breathe, and my tummy churns, and I feel all distant, as though I'm about to faint.'

'Mandy, you have to tell Steve the truth. He won't think any less of you.'

'Course he will. That Alice, she can do everything. She's going to be a violinist. She's already got an audition with an orchestra. She's got tons of A levels and so has Steve. And look at me. Just a chocolate-making apprenticeship.' Mandy sniffed. 'I don't mean to be rude about your business...'

'It's OK. I know what you mean.'

'When we argued, he looked at me like I was stupid.'

'Oh, Mandy. If I had a pound every time my husband made me feel foolish...' Libby's voice trailed away. She'd let Trevor call her stupid for years.

She looked across at Mandy's wet face. Her lodger wasn't going to suffer as she had; not if Libby had anything to do with it. 'If he insults you, he's not worth bothering with.'

'He didn't say it, exactly.' Mandy leapt to Steve's defence. 'I just know he's thinking it.'

Libby gave Mandy a hug. 'You daft thing. Don't imagine you know what someone else is thinking. Nobody can read minds. Now, let's do some more practice, you pass your test, and we'll think about how to get your hands on a little car. Maybe the business could manage something...'

Mandy rubbed her nose on her sleeve. 'You don't have to...'

'Let's get you through the driving test, first, shall we? We'll deal with the other stuff later. You could find someone to help you with the claustrophobia.'

Libby managed to sound calm, but she was worried. How long had Mandy been suffering from panic attacks? Did her mother, Elaine, now living quietly in Bristol after splitting with Mandy's violent father, know? Maybe Libby should call her. Or, was it none of her business?

She slumped back in her seat. Another problem to think about. Sometimes, it seemed solving murders was the least of her worries.

10

JOE

'Joe.' Max's son was on her doorstep on time the next morning, arm raised to pound on the door. 'You'd better come inside. It's freezing, out here.'

Libby pulled her dressing gown tight. She'd overslept, waking to the hammering on her front door. 'Couldn't you just ring the bell, like normal people do? Or is this an emergency?'

'Sorry. There's something I thought you'd like to know. I'm on my way to the station, so I can't stop.' Libby nodded, guessing he didn't want Chief Inspector Arnold to know he was calling on her.

She led him into the kitchen, flicking light switches as she went. 'Coffee? I need one before you tell me anything.'

Joe sniffed the air. Mandy must have fried bacon. 'What have you been cooking up?'

'Arsenic sandwiches,' Libby said. 'Want one?'

Joe snorted. 'Toast and Marmite would be good.'

Libby threw a couple of slices of bread in the machine. 'Watch that,' she ordered. 'It burns.'

Meekly, Joe oversaw toast while she fetched butter and

Marmite. Settled comfortably at the counter, he explained. 'We've got a suspect for the murder.'

'My, that was quick. Chief Inspector Arnold will be impressed.'

'It's his suspect.'

Libby paused, and butter slid from the tip of her knife. 'By which you mean, I suppose, that he's got the wrong man?'

Joe nodded and glanced round the room, looking as guilty as if he expected his boss to appear. 'It's not a man…'

Libby interrupted. 'Let me guess. It's a member of the Knitters' Guild?'

Joe frowned. 'Not just any member. It's your friend, Angela Miles.'

Libby dabbed Marmite on toast, buying time to think. It hadn't taken long for the police to discover Angela's connection with Giles Temple.

She tried to smile. 'That's ridiculous.' Her voice was a squeak.

Joe shook his head. 'Not really. It's the scarf, you see. Mrs Miles told the police she made it for Giles Temple as a present.' Libby breathed out. Angela had done the right thing and gone to the authorities, saving Libby that unpleasant task. She could concentrate on proving her friend's innocence.

She jabbed a finger at Joe. 'And when Angela killed the victim, she made sure the scarf was round his neck so everyone would suspect her? That's crazy. It won't stand up in court. Any decent lawyer will make mincemeat of the idea.'

Joe grimaced. 'The chief inspector wants someone in custody as soon as possible. He needs a success to show the press.'

'The police won't find any real evidence, because Angela didn't kill Giles Temple. You'll have to release her and then you'll look ridiculous.'

Joe nodded and Libby's breathing returned to normal. Joe

knew Angela Miles, and he was a smart man. He wouldn't be easily misled. 'I'd rather stop that happening, but there's a lot of police time focused on establishing evidence against Mrs Miles rather than following other leads. I'd send my team out, but my hands are tied. I thought you might have spare time...'

'You mean, when I'm not struggling with orders for chocolates, planning Robert's wedding, sorting out Mandy's problems or finding lost cats?'

Joe held up his hands. 'Angela's your friend.'

Libby heaved a sigh and poured more coffee. 'Of course, I'll do what I can to help. Let's look at the facts. For one thing, Giles Temple was strangled. That would take some strength. I can't imagine the middle-aged ladies of the Guild overcoming a healthy man in a struggle.'

Joe was nodding. 'I agree. Go on. What else do you think?'

'I think the scarf was planted to lay suspicion on the Knitters' Guild, or on Angela herself. The members of the Guild are mad as a bag of ferrets, but I can't see them wanting to kill Giles Temple.'

She paused. After a moment's thought, she shrugged. Time to share Vera's gossip. 'There's one person who might merit a closer look. Have you met the Dean's wife?'

'Chief Inspector Arnold sent Filbert-Smythe, our new detective sergeant with a first class degree from a swanky university, to interview the Dean and Mrs Weir. We won't be getting anything useful from that; I can guarantee it.'

Joe rolled his eyes. Filbert-Smythe's Oxbridge accent had not endeared him to the local police force, but he'd impressed Chief Inspector Arnold. 'The lad will be fine, once he gets some experience and stops brown nosing the bosses,' was Joe's verdict.

Libby blew out her cheeks, thinking hard. Should she tell Joe the big secret? She made up her mind. She wanted him to share information, so she must do the same. 'The Guild have a big event coming up in Wells. It's supposed to be a secret, but I think you should know.'

Joe groaned. 'Not a Greenham Common-type protest – sitting down in the streets?'

Libby laughed. 'This is a celebration. Do you remember the scaffolding at the cathedral? It was there for months.' Joe nodded. 'Now the work on the West Front's finished, they're planning a celebration. I'll tell you about it if you promise not to whisper it to a soul.'

'Cross my heart, so long as there's no danger to the public. Go on, you can't stop now.'

'The Guild members plan to smother the centre of Wells with knitting. They'll hang scarves from lamp posts, leave hats and gloves on benches and wrap blankets round trees. It's called yarn-bombing.'

'I've heard of it.'

'The bombs can be useful things, like mittens and ear warmers, and people are free to take them home. They'll leave silly stuff like toys and dolls as well, just for fun.'

'Do I need to request extra policing?'

'Well, they're not planning to do any damage and I can't imagine there'll be unmanageable crowds. Come along and see it. I imagine it'll be quite a sight.'

Joe's face was a picture. 'I wouldn't miss it for the world. In return, you'll help?'

Libby shrugged. 'I can't let Angela be a scapegoat, but you need to let me in on the evidence.' Joe hesitated. Libby rose, collecting cups and plates. 'If not, I can't help. You know I can be trusted to keep my mouth shut.'

Joe smiled. 'As a reward for breakfast, I'll tell you what I can. We don't have results from forensics yet, apart from the approximate time of death. Apparently, the heating in the library goes off at seven and it gets cold very fast up there, so it's only an approximation. The pathologist calls it an educated guess. Anyway, the best suggestion remains between six and midnight, as we said at the press conference.'

'What time does the library close?'

'Five o'clock.'

'Did Giles Temple have a key?'

'No. The bursar has one, I believe, and so does the verger.'

'Are researchers left alone with the books?'

'Occasionally. A volunteer often sits by the door.'

Joe had a glint in his eye. He tapped a finger on the countertop. 'Here's the thing I shouldn't be telling you. There's been another researcher working in the library this week. An American by the name of Reg Talbot.'

The name rang a bell. Libby closed her eyes for a moment as she struggled to remember.

Got it! Max's friend and colleague.

She said, 'That's been kept quiet. Not even the knitters mentioned it.'

'There's some sort of politics involved. I'll be in serious trouble if the boss finds out I told you, so keep it quiet, won't you? I think he's a contender, but the chief says we're to move on.'

Libby sucked her lower lip. 'I wonder why.'

'The thing is,' Joe went on, 'I've met him before. He works with Dad.'

Libby nodded. They were thinking along the same lines. 'So, there may be trouble at the cathedral?'

'Hard to say. It could be genuine research of some sort.'

'Like research into the Pilgrim Fathers? Has anyone interviewed this American?'

'I'm scheduled to speak to him later today.'

'I suppose I couldn't – I mean, can I watch from outside the room?'

Joe shook his head. 'Sorry, no clearance. But I'll tell you what I can, within the proper limits.'

'Not many Americans visit this part of the world. I suppose he'll be easy to recognise when he speaks, because of the accent.' A big grin split Joe's face. 'Why are you laughing?'

'He's the most recognisable man I've seen in Somerset. He won't need to say a word. He's an African American, about seven feet tall and bald as a coot. Used to play basketball. He's fit – very fit.'

11

CAT WOMAN

The Cedars. Despite the grand name, Mrs Marchant's Wells home turned out to be a tiny two bedroom house in the middle of a small terrace, a few streets away from the cathedral. Libby checked the address, turned off the ignition and climbed out of the car, mentally reducing the fee she'd been about to charge. Whoever lived here was unlikely to be rich.

Mrs Marchant opened her door a few inches and peered at Libby through round John Lennon spectacles. A pungent smell crept through the gap.

Libby recoiled. 'I've come about your cat.' In the distance, a cacophony of wails and squeals suggested several animals shared the house. 'One of your cats.'

'You'd better come in, then.' Mrs Marchant closed the door with a sharp click. The chain rattled for a full minute before the door opened. As Libby stepped inside, the overpowering smell of cats caught in her throat. She coughed as discreetly as possible and followed the woman down a narrow, dark passage.

'Mind your feet.' Mrs Marchant waved at an oblong litter tray covering half the width of the passage. Libby trod with care, skidding on the light dressing of litter scattered over an expanse of ancient brown, cracked linoleum, saving herself with a hand on the wall. Her fingers stuck to the dull brown wallpaper.

'Elsie,' the woman shouted. A fat grey moggy appeared at the top of a short flight of stairs, green eyes twinkling through the gloom, and picked her way downstairs, sedate as a Victorian miss. She wound in and out of Libby's legs, purring.

Two medium sized tabbies, a tiny black kitten, and a big marmalade giant followed. 'How many cats do you have?' Libby untangled herself and stepped into a small kitchen to find two large cages full of cats. Every remaining inch of floor held bowls of water and cat food.

Mrs Marchant pulled the sides of a grey cardigan across her thin chest, retied the knot in a belt of the same material, and picked a tiny white kitten out of one of the cages. 'Lost count, m'dear. All strays, you know.' She spoke with the deep, cut-glass accent Libby remembered from the phone call. 'They come here when they're lost. Impossible to keep count.'

The cats looked healthy and happy, but the smell was almost unbearable and Mrs Marchant's clothes struck Libby as shabby and threadbare. Beneath the cat stink, Libby detected the scent of unwashed garments. The woman was painfully thin. 'Cup of tea?'

Libby glanced at the sink where dirty dishes teetered in a pile and cracked mugs lay tumbled on the draining board. 'No, thanks. I can't stop long. You rang about a missing cat?'

'Oh yes, Mildred. She went out a few nights ago. Hasn't been back.'

'Was she a stray, too?'

'That's right, she's lived with me for a year or so. All my darlings are strays, except Emily, here.' She dropped the white kitten back in its cage and picked up the plump grey Emily, addressing the next remarks to the cat. 'You were my first cat, weren't you, my love. You came with me when I moved. We used to live in a lovely house called The Cedars. Just brought two things with me, don't you know – the name and the cat.'

Mrs Marchant put Emily down on a kitchen counter, where the animal picked a delicate route among teetering piles of tins, purring. 'Anyway, mustn't keep you. There's a picture of Mildred – the one that's lost – in one of these drawers.'

She moved to a shabby brown cabinet and pulled open one drawer after another. Scraps of paper, pens, spoons and elastic bands cascaded to the floor. Libby bent to retrieve them, trying not to touch the grubby floor. 'Here it is.'

The photo Mrs Marchant pushed under Libby's nose showed a plumper self, looking down an aristocratic nose at the camera. Libby, surprised, barely noticed the cat. 'Who took the photo?'

'My son. Terence.' She tossed the photo back in the drawer.

'Has he been here, lately?' Did he know his mother was living in squalor?

Mrs Marchant's eyes narrowed. 'Huh. What does he care? Children,' she glared, and Libby caught a brief glimpse of the handsome, haughty woman of the photo, 'are ungrateful little beasts.'

Surprised by such sudden vehemence, Libby's curiosity took over. 'Ungrateful?' she prompted.

'His father left everything to Terence on the understanding he'd look after me. Instead, what did my dear son do? Sold the house out from under my feet and left me in this place.'

'Does he realise you need help?' Mrs Marchant was a difficult and demanding woman, but surely no son would leave their mother in this state. She must have gone downhill fast and Terence deserved to be told. 'Where does he live?'

'Can't remember. Not far. Thirty miles or so.' Mrs Marchant gave an elaborate shrug. 'Lost the address, didn't I? Last time he came to see me was just after Mildred arrived. The day he took the photograph.' Libby groaned, inwardly. She couldn't let this state of affairs continue. She'd have to challenge Terence.

The temptation to walk away almost overwhelmed Libby. She could refuse the commission, leave Mrs Marchant to find her own cat, and forget about the ungrateful son. She already felt like a size eight foot in a size six shoe.

Instead, she added the task to her long mental to-do list and asked, 'May I keep Mildred's photo?' The cat woman shrugged, pulled it from the drawer among another shower of odds and ends, and handed it over.

'Has she been lost before?'

'Of course not. Well, just one night, shut in a neighbour's garage. She's not there now. I looked.'

The smell in the house sickened Libby. She had to get away. 'I'll arrange for some prints of the photo and distribute them around Wells. Would you like me to put an ad in the local paper? It might be expensive.'

'You may do as you wish. The cost,' Mrs Marchant raised both eyebrows, looking down the aristocratic nose at such vulgar talk of money, 'is of no consequence.'

12

SAMANTHA

The news of Angela Miles' interview under caution had travelled fast. On Thursday morning, half the inhabitants of Exham on Sea discovered they needed a loaf of bread or a cake, and Libby tuned in to every conversation, listening hard.

Gladys had been at school with Angela. 'She wouldn't harm a fly, and that's a fact.'

'Who knows.' The estate agent slouched by the counter. 'Middle-aged women—'

The florist cut him off, standing full square, hands on hips, eyes blazing. 'Middle-aged women what?'

'Nothing.' He backed away, stammering. 'I just meant she might be lonely. You know. Living alone. Maybe this Giles Temple took advantage of her.' He edged towards the door.

Mandy held out a paper bag. 'Don't forget your sandwich.' Red faced, he grabbed it and shot out of the shop, narrowly avoiding a collision with Samantha Watson.

'Well, really. Some people have no manners.' Patting her hair into place, the solicitor stalked to the counter to order smoked trout with mustard.

'It seems your friend Angela Miles is our killer, Libby. I'm surprised you missed that. You're supposed to be the local sleuth. But you're an amateur, of course. Perhaps you'll leave inquiries to the professionals, in future. Chief Inspector Arnold tells me the evidence against Mrs Miles is most compelling.'

Mandy slapped the solicitor's food on the counter. 'You mean that scarf?' she scoffed. 'Planted. Any fool can see that.'

Samantha sneered. 'You mind your manners, Mandy. If I had your background, I'd be more careful what I said.'

The spiteful words dropped into horrified silence. Someone drew a sharp breath. Mandy's father had been in trouble with the police many times. He'd even attacked her mother and threatened Mandy. Her face twisted in fury, mouth working, she escaped into the back kitchen.

Before Libby could gather her wits, Frank made a rare public appearance. Hiding in the back, he'd heard every word. He strode to the front door, held it open, glared at Samantha, and pointed to the street. 'You've gone too far, this time. Get out. You won't be served here in future.'

Samantha gasped. 'I haven't paid, yet.'

Frank folded his arms and waited as she picked up her food, tossed a handful of coins on the counter and swept out. At the door, she stopped. 'I won't forget this. Since you came here, Libby Forest, there's been nothing but trouble. Just watch out, you and your lodger. You'll be sorry.'

As the door slammed, the hubbub in the shop swelled. 'Well,' Gladys whispered to Libby, with a wary glance at Frank, 'if your apprentice dresses like a Goth, it's hardly surprising people think the worst.'

As the last customer left, Libby confided in Mandy and Frank. 'Sometimes I think a small town's the most vicious place in the world.'

Mandy scowled. 'Samantha Watson's got it coming. She's the one who'll be sorry.'

* * *

After the morning's drama, Libby took time alone to work in the peace of her kitchen while Mandy stayed at the bakery. Developing overdue new product lines, she forgot everything except her recipes.

Max would be home soon. It would be a relief to talk over the problems with him. 'I like my independence,' she explained to Bear and Fuzzy as she scraped food into separate bowls – fish for Fuzzy, beef for Bear, 'but I do miss him.'

Perhaps their partnership really could work. She stopped work for a moment, imagining it. If they set up as private investigators, she'd have to do a course, take exams. Butterflies swooped in her stomach, but it would be interesting. She liked a challenge. As for marriage? She shook her head. She'd think about that later. Max hadn't offered a proper proposal. A vague suggestion in a phone call didn't count.

Soon she was humming above the noise of mixer and grinder. Chocolate hearts needed filling. Libby mixed and measured, tested and tasted, until strawberry, coconut, lime, coffee and praline cream scented the air with heady sweetness and every chocolate brimmed with flavour.

She polished the kitchen until the surfaces shone, made a cheese sandwich and put her feet up. The living room reminded her of the last time Max sprawled on the sofa, Bear at his feet, stroking Fuzzy with one hand and twirling a whisky glass with the other, watching as an inch of golden liquid coated the sides.

Libby rarely sat here on her own. 'For heaven's sake,' she muttered. 'I'm getting sentimental.'

She pulled out a pair of knitting needles and a ball of wool she'd brought home from the Guild, curled up on the sofa and concentrated on producing squares. The Knitters' Guild would meet again, tomorrow, and Libby would be there.

If only Chief Inspector Arnold hadn't burst into the meeting, full of pomposity and self-importance, Libby might have discovered an important clue amongst the gossip. What had the knitters said? A vague thought, shapeless but insistent, nagged at Libby's brain. She couldn't bring it into focus. Maybe it would become clearer tomorrow.

13

DINNER

That evening, Libby felt like a mother hen with a brood of unruly chicks. Max had returned, but instead of the quiet evening together in the cottage she'd have preferred, they were eating supper at his almost-mansion, and were not alone.

Apart from Bear, snoring loudly in the corner of the room, there was Reg, Max's American colleague. Max wanted to introduce him to Libby. She suspected Max felt awkward after their phone call, and he'd brought his friend along as a buffer. Still, Libby wanted to know more about Reg's work in the cathedral library.

Max had sweetened the deal further by inviting Libby's son, Robert, his fiancée, Sarah, and Mandy. They'd arrived yesterday to stay with her parents for a few days. Sarah, a statuesque blonde, bubbly and excited, was full of wedding arrangements, but Robert had a different agenda. He told Libby he wanted to meet her 'friend'.

Libby hadn't yet confessed that Max was more than a friend.

Joe, though invited, had not come. He was on duty. Had that been an excuse? Libby hoped not. The relationship between

father and policeman son had been strained since Max divorced
Joe's mother, many years ago. Things had improved recently, and
Libby prided herself on helping smooth the path with input to
some of Joe's cases.

Since that angry scene in the bakery, Mandy had been
subdued, answering questions with monosyllables. When Libby
suggested she might like to attend Max's homecoming dinner,
she'd pretended indifference. Libby turned away. 'Max asked me
to invite you, but it's your choice.'

That did the trick. Mandy tossed her head and mumbled but
she wore a sheepish grin and sounded far perkier as she said,
'You need me there to stop you talking about weddings and
boring business all evening.'

To Libby's surprise, Mandy had toned down her appearance
for the occasion and looked stunning in one of Libby's silk
blouses over a pair of velvet trousers.

Max welcomed the guests with champagne. He discarded his
apron with a flourish, as though he'd spent hours in the kitchen.
In fact, the meal had come straight from Libby's freezer along
with simple instructions.

'Reg's just taking a call,' he explained. 'He'll be down in a
minute – Ah, here he is. Reg, let me introduce you to some of my
neighbours and friends.'

Libby heard Mandy's sharp intake of breath and glanced sideways. The girl's mouth hung half open. Libby swallowed a
chuckle. She didn't blame Mandy; Reg was gorgeous. He was tall
enough even to dwarf Max, his body was lean and fit looking, and
his skin glowed the warm colour of a summer tan. It was hard to
assess his age; mid-thirties, perhaps. His head was clean-shaven.
Libby disliked that fashion, but she could make an exception in
Reg's case.

They shared small talk. 'I love your British weather,' Reg said.

'In my part of Texas, it's pretty much the same every day. Hot. Here, you never know what's coming. One day it's freezing, and the next you have this gentle rain.'

Max ushered them into the dining room. 'We call it drizzle.'

'The sun does shine occasionally.' Libby defended her home country.

Bear followed close behind. 'You know, I think he misses Fuzzy,' Max said, 'or Shipley.'

Robert said, 'I haven't met the notorious Shipley. Didn't he help you find the body under the lighthouse?'

'He did. I used to walk him when I first arrived in Exham. Since his owners left, he lives with the vet, hoping for a new family.'

She smiled at Sarah. 'Any takers?'

'Don't look at us. Once we're married, we might think about a dog, or maybe a cat. Robert's more of a cat person. But we need to settle down, first. With all the wedding preparations, everything seems a whirl just now.'

Libby kept an eye on Mandy. Seated opposite Reg, she'd focused her dark, kohl rimmed eyes on the American newcomer, from time to time tucking a stray lock of hair behind an ear. Maybe her gloom at Steve's defection would be short lived. Bear lay under the table, alert in case someone dropped a titbit.

Reg's biceps rippled inside a beautifully cut jacket as he stretched to offer Libby a dish of carrots roasted with cardamom and honey. 'Ma'am,' he drawled, his voice as warm and liquid as Nat King Cole's, 'I can tell Max didn't cook this up. I gather you're a professional, and I can tell why. I haven't had a meal like this in years. Why, those chefs in the city, dribbling little pools of sauce on inch long pieces of half cooked fish, ought to come out here for a few lessons.' Libby blushed, tried not to simper, and offered him a second, larger helping. 'You bet. A man my size needs a good meal.'

Robert said, 'Mum's meals were famous when I was at school. I had to rotate my friends, there were so many wanting to try her apple and ginger crumble.'

Sarah said. 'So that's how you got girls, in those days.' She leaned back in her chair, with a sigh. 'Maybe I shouldn't have eaten quite so much roast lamb. I should have saved myself for pudding.'

As the engaged couple shared smiles, their eyes on each other, Libby glanced at Reg, wondering at his interest in Giles Temple's death.

Max had insisted Libby could trust his colleague. 'I've known him for years and he's spent a long time in England. He read for a research degree at Cambridge University, something about the crossover between history and science. He likes to play up his deep south accent when he's around women, though. They swoon.'

Now she'd met him, Libby understood why. 'We still meet up from time to time when I'm in the States or he's in England.' Max had said. 'We're pretty much in the same business.'

Reg tucked into his second helping of Libby's special roast lamb and launched into an explanation of his presence in Somerset. His story was plausible and Libby relaxed a little. She'd been anxious about Robert meeting Max and Reg. She wanted to avoid involving her son and his fiancée in any undercover work, but Reg's task sounded straightforward. 'The cathedral library has some unique and ancient books, donated over the centuries by what you British call 'canons' at the cathedral. Don't you love the idea of religious men named after weapons?' Mandy's eyes were fixed in transparent adoration on the speaker. Max winked at Libby.

Reg continued, 'Why, there was a book there, from the sixteenth century, that used to belong to your Thomas Cranmer—you know, Archbishop of Canterbury when Henry VIII was king? There are notes he wrote himself. How about that?'

Max said, 'The question everyone will ask, Reg, is whether you were in the library on the night of the murder?' There was a pause, and the air grew tense, as though everyone around the table realised the implication of the question. Was Reg a suspect? Even Robert's gaze shifted to the American.

Reg sighed. 'You always were a straight talker, my friend. No, I was travelling down from my temporary office in Bristol and staying at the Swan, sampling your local brew; Butcombe Gold, I seem to recall. I think the bar staff at the hotel will back me up.'

Everyone relaxed a fraction. Reg looked from one face to another. 'Here's something you may be interested in.' He addressed Libby. 'I can tell you about the book it seems Giles Temple was reading. The police mentioned it to me, wanting to know if I'd looked at it.'

'What was it?' Mandy asked.

'A travel guide, full of maps of the world. At least, the world they knew in the seventeenth century. Not the most precious book in the collection, but still worth a pretty penny.'

Libby's mind raced. 'How do you know that's the book he was reading?'

Max said, 'It's a best guess, according to Joe Ramshore, but the police can't be sure. Giles Temple wore white gloves in the library to avoid acid from his fingers damaging some of the books, so there are no recent fingerprints, but the spine of this one stuck out a bit from the others, as though someone in a hurry had shoved it back on the shelf. That attracted the police officer's attention.'

'The murderer left the book behind? Isn't that odd?' Libby

was thinking aloud. 'Why did he shove it back so carelessly? Didn't that just draw attention to it?'

Her voice trailed away as Robert queried, 'Why do you keep saying "him" for the murderer? Are you sure it was a man?'

Max nodded. 'Good question. Joe thinks it's likely. The victim was strangled with a chain, so the murderer was strong. It would take plenty of force to keep the pressure on the chain with the victim fighting for his life.' Libby winced. 'But I guess a fit woman could manage, if she took him by surprise.'

He added, 'There's something else. Chains, like the one used to strangle Mr Temple, are attached to the shelves in the library with forged steel bolts. The murderer must have brought along some hefty bolt cutters.'

'Which means,' Robert interrupted, excited, 'he had a plan. He came prepared to kill Giles Temple that night.'

14

GHOSTS

Robert and Sarah left, arms entwined, taking a taxi to Sarah's parents' home. They were still chattering about the murder.

A lump formed in Libby's throat as she stood with Max in the doorway, watching. It seemed that only yesterday Robert had been a little boy, holding Libby's hand as they walked to the park.

She leaned on Max's shoulder. 'They're almost as excited about the mystery as their wedding. Still, it's very strange to see your son with another woman. Sarah will come first in his life, from now on.'

He slipped an arm round her shoulders. 'That's how it should be. You must be proud of Robert. He does you credit.'

'I am. I used to think he was dull until Sarah brought him out of his shell. Funny, how wrong you can be about your own children. I suppose it was the contrast with Ali – she was the enthusiast, always dreaming up new projects. I never knew what she was going to do next. I shouldn't have been surprised when she left university so abruptly and dashed off to South America. At least, judging by her emails, she's forgiven me for disapproving.'

Max sounded rueful. 'It's so hard to get it right when you have children. I made every mistake possible with mine. If I'd known my daughter would have that riding accident and die so young, I'd have spent every moment with her, instead of working away from home so often.'

Libby said, 'We can't change our natures. Look at you, still working when you could be happily retired on your banking pension.'

'But what would I do all day? At least Joe and I are talking again. I wish he'd been here tonight, to meet Robert. Still, there'll be time for that. He's pleased about you and me, you know. It's almost enough to make him forgive me for the past.'

Libby leaned against Max. 'I'm pleased, too.'

'But not enough for marriage?'

'Not quite yet. Give me time. Let's go back and see how the other pair are doing.'

Mandy and Reg were tidying Max's kitchen, Reg explaining the rules of basketball while Mandy listened, open mouthed. Max whispered, 'More love-birds.'

Mandy's face glowed. She had a wine glass in each hand. 'Reg wants to know if this house is haunted.'

Max snorted. 'Don't listen to him, Mandy. Reg sees ghosts everywhere. It's his hobby.'

Mandy and Libby spoke in unison, breathless. 'Really?'

Max sighed. 'It's one of his ploys to attract women. Successful, of course.'

'That's very sexist,' Mandy objected.

'Maybe, but true. Anyway, Reg, it looks like you've already hooked these two.' Max rescued a wine glass from Mandy's grasp as she drained the other. 'You'd better explain. What makes you think I have a ghost? I can't say I've seen anyone cross the hall with his head beneath his arm.'

Reg pointed to Bear. 'You can scoff, but that dog senses something. There are parts of this house that bother him. He followed me down the hall just now, stopped at the third door and wouldn't go in.'

Libby admitted, 'I've noticed it, too. It's the drawing room that bothers him. Sometimes he won't pass the door at all. He just pokes his nose in and backs right away to the kitchen.'

Max led them into his comfortable, scruffy study. Reg stretched out in an armchair, his legs reaching halfway across the room. 'I had no idea you had a drawing room, Max. I thought it was something only your British royalty would own.'

'It comes with the house. I'll admit I hardly go in. It's far too formal. I just use it when I want to impress someone like the Lord Lieutenant on official business.'

Reg scratched his head. 'You Brits and your aristocracy; I'm not even going to ask what a Lord Lieutenant is. But I'd love to have a peek in the drawing room. Come on now, back me up, Mandy.'

'I've never been somewhere as posh as a drawing room,' Mandy giggled. 'We just had a front room, where I grew up. Should I call you Lord Ramshore?'

Libby joined in. 'Come on, Max. Haven't you ever wondered about ghosts? This is such an old house.'

Max grinned. 'Are you sure you want to start ghost hunting? You'll give yourself nightmares. You were scared enough that time you were lost on Glastonbury Tor.'

'Don't try and get out of it that way. Come on, spill the beans.'

'Okay, then, here's the story. I'll start it properly. Once upon a time...'

Mandy chortled. Max winked at her and continued. 'Once upon a time I sat in there, reading. It was soon after I moved into the house, half a dozen years ago. I was reading Dickens. Great Expectations, I think. Seemed appropriate in an old pile like this.

Anyway, it was midsummer, on one of the three hot days we had that year. We call that a heat wave, Reg, by the way.'

Reg laughed, but Mandy complained, 'Get back to the story.'

'Sorry. I realised my feet were freezing cold. It felt as though they had ice packed round them. The rest of me was fine, even a bit too warm. I got up to walk around, warm the toes up a bit, and,' his voice dropped to a whisper, 'I felt something cold land on my shoulder.'

Mandy gasped. 'Like a hand?'

He nodded; his face solemn. 'It was heavy, like a dead weight. I looked round, but there was nothing to be seen. I told myself I was imagining things and tried to go on reading, but my feet just got colder. I told myself, "Don't be ridiculous. It's just a draught." These old buildings have plenty of spots where the wind gets through, even with half decent central heating. I moved across and sat in another chair, but...'

Mandy put in, 'The cold spot followed you?' She licked her lips, eyes shining.

Libby leaned forward, caught up in the story. 'What happened next?'

'Nothing. In the end, I went back into my study to get warm.'

Mandy groaned. 'That can't be the end. Was Bear with you then?'

'No, it was before I inherited him. You're right, though, Libby. He's never gone into that room. This old house has plenty of other places he prefers.'

Mandy's eyes glowed. 'Did it happen again?'

'Every time I sit in there, to tell the truth.'

Libby grinned at Mandy. 'Come on. We have to investigate this, even though I don't believe a word of it. There's nothing to beat a good ghost story. Let's go into the drawing room, right now, and see what happens.'

Max led the way down the corridor. Bear padded beside Libby, as far as the door. Max pushed on the wood. Slowly, it creaked open and Mandy gasped. Bear stopped; his legs rigid. Mandy whispered, 'He doesn't like it here, does he?'

The dog barked, once. His tail drooped and the ruff of fur round his neck stood on end. He managed to look miserable and offended at the same time. Max strode into the middle of the room and held out a dog treat. 'Come on, Bear.' The dog took a step forward, hesitated, looked from Libby to Max, barked again, turned and padded back along the corridor.

'Does that count as proof?' Libby asked, an odd feeling in the pit of her stomach.

Max took her hand. 'Come on, Reg, you're the expert. Is there a ghost in here?'

Reg paced round the room, stopping at intervals, his face serious. 'There's a strange atmosphere,' he concluded. 'There are cold spots, just as you described. Are there any records of odd happenings? Witches in the area?'

'Nothing I've been able to track down. I've looked at various histories of the house and the surrounding area, but I haven't managed to turn up anything interesting apart from the Battle of Sedgemoor.'

Reg beamed from ear to ear. 'While I'm here, maybe I can do a little research into your local history. Tell me about this battle.'

Max wrinkled his brow. 'The Duke of Monmouth was a pretender to the throne of England, back in the eighteenth century. He landed in the West Country, fought the king's army and was defeated. Most of his followers died, and the rest ran away.'

'Maybe some got this far...'

'Before they died...' Reg and Mandy were talking over each other, Mandy's face pink with happiness.

* * *

Libby, Mandy and Reg stayed at Max's house that night. They sat up, drinking coffee, until late into the night. Max looked out of the window. 'It's freezing cold out there and I doubt you could see your hand in front of your face. Just the weather to give Bear his final walk. Coming, Libby?'

Bear appeared, miraculously, at the door. He'd been out of sight, most likely curled up in the room Max grandly called the gun room. Libby had never seen a gun in the house. Did Max own one? He'd never told her. Just one more thing she'd find out one day. She stood up, slightly tipsy. 'Wellington boots and hats needed, I think.'

No one else would leave the warmth of the blazing fire for the cutting blast of winter's east winds. Libby and Max trudged, arm in arm, down the lane, the wind in their faces, using a flashlight to avoid the worst of the puddles. 'I know you trust Reg, but do you think we should have talked about the murder so much?'

'Why, because Joe thinks he's a suspect?' Max scoffed. 'Joe's not a fool, even if his chief is. He interviewed Reg this afternoon and the alibi checks out. He was travelling all that day, with train tickets to back him up, and the woman behind the bar remembers him being there all evening. He's very distinctive, as you've seen. She almost melted while talking about him. He's been eliminated from the enquiry.'

'That's just as well. Did you see Mandy's face? I think she's in love.' She told Max about Mandy's quarrel with Steve. 'She's got this enormous inferiority complex, and it's making her miserable and jealous. I'm worried about her, to be honest.'

'You're doing all you can. Let her be. She has to make her own mistakes.'

15

GUILT

After a morning baking and an afternoon struggling with a pair of unruly knitting needles, Libby was ready for the next meeting of the Knitters' Guild. Ignoring the uneven edges of her squares, Libby stuffed them into a bag, pulled on her thickest woollen sweater, a pair of jeans and sheepskin lined boots, persuaded the engine of the Citroen to kick into action on the third attempt, and drove through the murk of a dark winter's evening.

The car sped along deserted lanes, round twists and turns. Libby loved to drive in the dark, able to see the lights of an approaching car well before it arrived. Tonight, though, the darkness seemed less dense. It would be hours before dawn broke, but the sky grew brighter every moment. Libby slowed, puzzled.

She turned another corner. Between the naked arms of a leafless hedgerow a gleam of bright orange flickered. Libby drove closer and sniffed the air. An acrid, bitter smell filled the car. The smell of fire.

Smoke billowed, a patch of denser black against the sky. One more turn in the lane and Libby saw the fire straight ahead, bright against the night sky. With a shock of horror, she recognised the isolated eighteenth century thatched cottage where Samantha Watson lived.

She screeched to a halt, leapt from the car and ran through a gate in the white painted fence, towards the house. A light shone from one of the upstairs rooms. 'No. oh no. Samantha must be in there.' No face appeared at the window.

Searing heat beat her back. She gasped for breath; lungs full of smoke.

The fire brigade. Coughing, she grabbed the phone from her pocket and fumbled, fingers trembling, for the emergency button, bellowing the news, the roar of fire threatening to drown her voice.

Help was on its way, but the fire had taken hold and black smoke billowed from the front door. Where was Samantha? Was she inside? Why hadn't she run out? Sick with fear, Libby ran round the cottage, searching for a way in, but the fire burned even more fiercely at the back.

She shrieked Samantha's name, but all she heard in reply was the shatter of glass as a window exploded high above, driving Libby back. Glass showered like snow into the garden.

Water. She needed water to drown the flames. Desperately, she scanned the garden, the unnatural light of the fire delineating every detail. A tiny stream trickled along beside a wall, but she had no way of carrying the water. She needed a bucket. Where could she find one?

A shed stood halfway down the garden, out of range of the fire. Libby rattled the door, but it was locked. She kicked the lock once. It trembled but held. She took a run at the door and crashed painfully against the wood.

The wail of a fire engine sounded, ever closer. Libby took another hopeless run at the shed. Hands grabbed at her arms, pulling her back. 'Leave it to us, now.'

'Thank heaven, you're here.' Howling with frustration, she screamed, 'I think Samantha's in there. It's her house and the light was on. I couldn't get in...'

She broke off, paralysed, as with a roar like a steam train, the thatched roof threw a volcano of fire into the air and collapsed, tumbling into the house.

Someone led Libby away. 'There's nothing you can do. We can't get in until the fire's under control. Keep back while the lads work.'

Sobbing, she sank to the ground as fire officers unrolled a heavy hose. A torrent of water flooded the house, until every inch was drenched. Slowly, the flames flickered and died.

For Libby, time seemed to stand still. The house was a shell, no more than four blackened walls, when at last two burly figures pushed their way through the space where the door used to stand.

Libby held her head in her hands, tears rolling down her cheeks, waiting and hoping, knowing it was impossible for Samantha to have survived the inferno, praying she'd been away from home.

The fire officers returned, shoulders drooping. An officer trudged across to Libby and removed a heavy helmet. Libby recognised a young woman who often came into the bakery. Libby didn't know her name. *Cheese and pickle baguette. That's what she buys.* Libby's thoughts shied away from the truth she read in the woman's face.

'I'm sorry, Mrs Forest.' The officer wiped a sweaty forehead with the back of her hand. 'You're right. There's someone in there.'

Libby shuddered, horror clutching her stomach. Voice trembling, she asked the question, knowing the answer already. 'Is she dead?'

'I'm so sorry.'

'Anyone else?' had Chief Inspector Arnold been there with her?

Libby closed her eyes and sank to the ground, hardly aware of the freezing water that puddled on the lawn, soaking her jeans. 'If I'd been here sooner. If I hadn't had that last cup of coffee...'

The officer crouched at her side. 'You did all you could. Are you hurt?'

Libby shook her head, turned away and emptied the contents of her stomach on the muddy ground.

* * *

She threw her clothes into a black bin bag and dumped it in her spare room. She'd never wear them again. She showered, scrubbing every inch of her body under hot water, and shampooed her hair three times. The smell of burning lingered everywhere, in her chest and throat, in the pores of her skin. It filled the cottage.

She gargled with mouthwash and sprayed the house with Glade. All the while, a voice in her head whispered, 'You never liked Samantha Watson.' No matter how hard Libby tried, she couldn't subdue that small, persistent voice of guilt.

Max helped her onto the sofa and handed over a glass of brandy. He'd found the bottle under the sink. It had belonged to her husband. Libby hated brandy, but tipped a big slug down her throat, anyway. Maybe it would banish the smell of smoke. 'Are you feeling better?' Max asked.

She tried to smile. 'A little. My conscience is working overtime. Samantha said there's been nothing but trouble since I came to Exham. I wonder if she was right?'

'Nonsense. That's delayed shock talking. Why should the fire be your fault? You had nothing to do with it. In fact, you nearly rescued Samantha.'

'I'm afraid 'nearly' wasn't enough.' Libby shuddered. 'That chocolate-box thatched roof looked cute, but wasn't the house a disaster just waiting to happen?'

Max tucked a rug around her knees. 'In fact, thatched roofs are no more combustible than other materials, but so many things can start a fire. Candles left burning, or gas, or a cigarette.'

'Samantha didn't smoke. I don't understand why she didn't get out when the fire started'

'Who knows. Maybe she wanted an early night, perhaps had a couple of drinks that made her woozy. Once a fire takes hold, it's amazing how fast it travels. It's usually the smoke that chokes people, prevents them from escaping.'

Libby shuddered. 'What a terrible way to die. I suppose the police and fire service will be on the case, and we'll find out the full story.'

Max tried to refill her brandy glass, but she made a face and pushed it away.

He said. 'For one thing, they'll have the insurance company on their backs, trying to avoid a huge pay out. Samantha would have all the proper documentation. She was a solicitor, after all.' He frowned. 'Though any documents may have been destroyed in the fire.'

Libby struggled to sit up straight. 'There are sure to be electronic copies online.'

Max poured another slug of brandy into his glass. 'I'll bet super-efficient Samantha had a fireproof filing cabinet. Or if not, she might have left paperwork at the solicitors' office. Anyway, Chief Inspector Arnold will sort it out. Poor fellow.'

Libby shuddered. Those things she'd said about Samantha

and the chief inspector in the past; if only she could take them back. 'He'll be devastated. They've been engaged for months.'

She yawned and her eyelids drooped. The brandy was doing its job. 'I'm going to bed. I can't think any more tonight. It's been such a week, what with Giles Temple, and Angela, and that scene in the shop, and...' She stopped, half way to the door, with a sharp intake of breath.

'What is it?' Max, gathering glasses, paused.

'Nothing. I just remembered...' Libby forced herself to breathe evenly. She tried a weary smile. 'It's nothing. I'm tired. Good night.'

She couldn't tell anyone, not even Max, about the picture in her head: the fury on Mandy's face and the venom in the words she'd hissed in Libby's ear as the solicitor left the bakery. 'She'll be sorry.'

16

GOSSIP

Libby woke late to find a rare beam of light flooding the room between the curtains. She rolled over and a mild pain behind her eyes intensified until her entire head throbbed. She scrubbed at her face, eyes squeezed shut, desperate to erase the memory of last night's fire.

She sat up, pulse racing, as she remembered Mandy's fury. Could her apprentice possibly have anything to do with the fire? Libby shuddered. Mandy would never, ever do such a thing. Of course, she wouldn't.

Libby paused to think. Yesterday was Mandy's day off. She'd muttered something about visiting friends before going to The Dark Side, the club frequented by Somerset's small Goth community, for the evening. Libby could easily check on her movements. All she had to do was talk to Mandy's friends.

She chewed her lip. Go behind her apprentice's back? What was she thinking? She must ask Mandy herself. She swung her legs out of bed, threw on a dressing gown, grabbed her phone and looked at the time. Too late. Mandy must have left the house by now.

Libby fought down a stab of panic. *Think logically.* She took a deep breath and sank on to the bed. There were plenty of other possible causes of the fire. A kitchen fire? The organised Samantha would have a fire blanket in the house. Candles, or a spark from an open hearth? Possibly. What about cigarettes? Samantha did not smoke, but maybe someone else had been with her earlier, dropping a lighted cigarette end behind a chair, or near a curtain, where it could smoulder, unnoticed, before bursting into flame. A single half extinguished cigarette could burn down a house.

Libby sighed. This was all hopeful nonsense. Controlling, superior Samantha would never let anyone smoke in her home, and the fire officers had only found one body.

Two suspicious deaths within a week was too much of a coincidence. They could be connected, and Libby wouldn't find the link by sitting upstairs all morning.

She sniffed as a tantalising smell crept into the room. Bacon. Max was making breakfast. How could she have forgotten Max that had stayed overnight in the third bedroom? Her heart suddenly light, she ran downstairs.

He waved her to a stool, set down a plate of bacon and eggs and clattered cutlery. 'How are you, this morning?'

Libby, ravenously hungry, smiled. 'Much better. You're turning into quite a chef. Has Mandy gone to work?'

'Haven't seen her. I don't think she was here last night.'

Without another word, Libby turned, ran upstairs, and threw open Mandy's door. The room was empty. Either Mandy had left so quietly no one heard her go, or she hadn't slept here last night.

Libby's appetite vanished. She played with breakfast, struggling to force down the food, making light of Mandy's absence. 'She sometimes stays with her friends overnight.'

She sent Max home, pleading a long list of cake commissions.

She needed to be alone to phone Mandy. She couldn't share her suspicions with Max at this stage. Not yet.

Max argued, but Libby was adamant. She had work to do. He swallowed the last of the bacon. 'If you're sure you feel OK.'

'Of course. I'm fine.' As he left, Libby's fears returned. She must speak to Mandy before she could relax. She fumbled in the diary with nervous fingers.

She ran a finger down the appointments. Mandy planned to visit Jumbles in Bath, today, discussing orders for Mrs Forest's Chocolates. Libby tried her apprentice's mobile, but it went to voice mail. She swore and tried again. Nothing. Mandy must be in the meeting already. Libby left a text message.

Ring me when you can. Need to talk. Urgent!

Near to tears, she threw the phone down, leaned on a table and buried her face in her hands.

A few long, slow breaths slowed her heart rate. Calm once more, she retrieved the phone and rang Angela's number. She could explain why she'd missed the meeting last night and talk over the horrible business of Samantha and the fire.

Angela let the call go to voice mail. Surely, the police couldn't have arrested her? But, that news would already have been around the town. Libby left a message. 'Sorry I missed the Knitters' Guild. Can we meet, later today?'

Libby's grabbed her phone as it pinged. Was it Mandy?

No, Angela. Libby read the message.

Can't talk just now. Meet later?

Libby would have to be patient. She drummed her hands on the table, frustrated, desperate for action – any action.

* * *

She showered once more, dressed in her oldest clothes, and drove out to Wells. She'd check on Mrs Marchant, to see if the cat had come home, letting Libby off the hook. She'd done almost nothing to find it, so far.

She rang the bell three times, but no one came to the door. Defeated, Libby shrugged and walked back to the car. Today was going from bad to worse.

'Libby Forest?' The hearty voice made her jump. Ruby, one of the knitters, appeared at her shoulder. 'Fancy meeting you here,' she beamed. 'I'm all alone this morning. How about a cup of coffee? Mrs Marchant's out. Taken one of her moggies to the vet, I expect. She loves those animals, bless her. Didn't know you knew her?'

Libby's spirits revived at the prospect of a dose of Ruby's cheerful gossip. 'You live near here?'

'Just over there. Vivian Marchant and I are old friends.'

She led Libby across the narrow road, flung open a red painted door and bustled inside, waving for Libby to follow.

The house, though similar in style to Mrs Marchant's, looked completely different. Floor to ceiling windows flooded the rooms with light, highlighting cushions, curtains and rugs in vibrant shades of purple and green. Libby admired a display of exotic indoor plants. 'Is that a bird of paradise plant?' Her knowledge of plants was worse than patchy, but the display was beautiful.

'My babies,' Ruby laughed. 'In winter, I can't work in the garden, so I keep plants in the house. My husband has his shed outside, to do his little bits of woodwork, but this room is mine.' She sighed. 'I can't wait to get back to my vegetable patch.'

'Your garden's very striking.' Libby joined Ruby at the window, to gaze across a space filled with a riot of bananas, palms and olive trees.

'I never want to go on holiday,' Ruby laughed. 'It's like a tropical island here. You couldn't grow these plants anywhere else in England, you know.' She laughed a good deal, and with every burst of merriment, her chins wobbled and bounced.

A pond near the house looked new. 'We dug that last summer, and we're letting it settle. In spring, we'll be adding the fish. Carp. You know, the fat ones?'

Libby nodded. 'I'd love a pond, but the ground's so heavy in my garden. I tried to dig but I got stuck a few inches down.'

'Oh, the clay! Yes, it took a few weeks to dig my pond. Practise, that's what you need. Take it slowly and build up a few muscles. It's worth it. My garden means everything to me, now my son's grown up.' Ruby's smile was sad. 'I miss him terribly. He left a gap in my life when he moved away, but he's always in my heart. I'd do anything for him. Do you have children?'

Libby told her about Ali, her daughter, saving the south American rain forest. 'My son's getting married soon,' she added, trying not to sound smug. 'In the cathedral.'

Ruby clasped her hands. 'Lucky, lucky you. I hardly see my son, these days. Just two or three times a year. I wish he'd bring a nice young lady home. Women have such a settling effect, don't you think?'

She sighed, her chest heaving. 'Still, mustn't grumble. I have all I want here, and he comes at Christmas. Now, let me get you some cake. Oh.' She collapsed in a chuckling heap on a chair. 'I suppose offering you cake is taking coals to Newcastle, as my mother used to say. Your cakes are famous. Look, I have your book.'

She sorted through a pile on a coffee table, repositioning illustrated gardening books and solid tomes on interior decorating, finally digging out *Baking at the Beach*. 'Would you sign it for me?'

Libby signed, in her usual untidy scribble, as Ruby wiped her eyes and heaved herself up. She disappeared into the kitchen, chuckling, and returned with a tray, still talking. 'Those cats, you know, over the way. Child substitutes. Did I mention that? Old Vivian Marchant drove her family away with her bad temper. The son never visits, not even at Christmas. She's on her own. Of course, Walter and I invited her here. There's always space for another neighbour beside a warm fire at Christmas, don't you agree? Our son was here, on one of his visits, but we could have squeezed a little one like Viv Marchant in. But she wouldn't have it.' Ruby fussed with plates, knives and paper napkins. 'Can't help some people, you know.'

She turned up the gas fire and the temperature rose. Sweating, Libby shrugged off her gilet. 'And another thing...' Libby longed to make notes of Ruby's unending chat, but fearing it might stem the flow of good-natured gossip, she tried to memorise every word instead. Her hostess, uninhibited, had a hint, an insinuation or a piece of downright scandal about everyone.

Ruby filled in the life and habits of every one of her neighbours and the regulars at the cathedral. 'I take flowers there, in the spring and summer. I always say, you can't have too many flowers in God's house. The Dean's wife tells me not to bother, I do too much already for the community, but I believe in giving, don't you? I can always spare time to help folk out.'

'The Dean's wife?' Libby prompted.

'Oh, yes, she's a special friend of mine, you know. "Ruby," she says. "We can always rely on you." Amelia's rather young for a Dean's wife, you know. Sometimes, she just needs a little hint.'

Libby nodded, schooling her face into seriousness, wondering whether the Dean's wife found Ruby overwhelming.

'I suspect there's been trouble in that house.' Ruby took a bite of cake, smudging a little cream on her upper lip. Libby tried not to stare. 'I'm afraid dear Amelia is just a little too welcoming to newcomers, if you get my drift. Especially gentlemen.'

She favoured Libby with a warm, conspiratorial grin. 'A very nice lady, of course. Very nice indeed. I've got a lovely anthurium I promised to give her. She adores the plants in this room, you see, and she wants to have something similar. They say imitation is the sincerest form of flattery, don't they?'

She laughed gaily. Libby, glad of the perfect excuse to talk to Amelia Weir, offered to help. 'Would you like me to deliver the plant for you? I'm going over that way.'

Ruby beamed, swooped on a plant nearby and pushed it into Libby's arms.

Libby, arms full of plant, took that as a signal to leave, but before she could move, the door opened. A bald head slid into view, whispering, 'Anything you want from the shops, dear?' A wiry body followed the head into the room.

'Walter,' Ruby cried. 'Where have you been all morning? In that poky old shed, I suppose, up to your usual nonsense.'

Walter shuffled closer and halted, one foot poised for escape. He shot a longing glance at the door. 'Just finishing that cloche you wanted, dear.' The gentle voice had a soft, Welsh lilt.

'This is Mrs Forest, the *Baking at the Beach* author. She's signed my book.'

He squinted at Libby. 'The famous Mrs Forest, is it? I've heard about your exploits. On the track of a mystery, are you? The killer at the cathedral?'

'I'm looking for a missing cat. It belongs to Mrs Marchant.'

'Not here, I'm afraid. Not allowed in the garden. Lion droppings, that's the answer. Get 'em from the internet, sprinkle on the flower beds. Works a treat.' He rubbed strong hands together. 'Not looking into this affair at the cathedral, then?'

'Sad business, isn't it?'

'So it is. Ah well, no peace for the wicked. Back to the grindstone.' Walter headed for the door and Libby grasped the opportunity to follow.

Ruby lurched to her feet, still chattering. 'We'll be on the lookout for stray cats, Walter and I. Always keen to help our neighbours. Isn't that right, Walter?'

He disappeared, the musical voice floating behind. 'Yes, dear.'

17

Amelia Weir seemed far from pleased to see her visitor. 'If you're looking for the Dean, he's in his office at the cathedral.' Her voice was distant and chilly.

Libby pasted the warmest smile she could manage on her face. 'I was just taking to Ruby. She wanted to send you this plant. It's an anthurium, apparently.'

Stony faced, the Dean's wife took the plant, and deposited it on a semi-circular table in the hall. 'Thank you for delivering it.' She smiled without showing her teeth. 'Ruby is far too generous.'

Amelia Weir was an attractive woman with dark brown hair. Chestnut lights reflected the glow from an impressive chandelier in the cavernous entrance hall. The Dean's second wife, according to Ruby, was many years younger than her widowed husband.

'I know who you are, Mrs Forest. I suppose you've decided to undertake an amateur investigation.' The Dean's wife folded her arms across her chest, the gesture uncertain, defensive. 'I expect you want to know about my relationship with Giles Temple.'

'If you're prepared to tell me, it would certainly save a lot of time.'

'I expect it's all over Wells by now. I was friendly with Giles Temple, but I'm sorry to have to disappoint you. My husband knows about it and there's no mystery.'

She watched Libby's face. Libby, keeping her expression blank, waited in silence. The Dean's wife clicked her tongue as if irritated and continued. 'Giles and I were at university together. Giles studied for a PhD while I was an undergraduate. We had a brief romance, just a few dates, but it didn't go anywhere. We stayed friends and kept in touch. He was happily married and so am I. Our relationship was no secret, and I didn't kill my old friend.'

Amelia's wide blue eyes looked Libby full in the face. Either she was telling the truth, or she was a very accomplished liar.

Libby began, 'I didn't say—'

Amelia interrupted. 'I expect your informants told you I met Giles for a drink a few days ago.' Libby smiled, hoping she looked enigmatic. 'We discussed my husband's birthday. He'll be sixty next month. Giles found a book my husband might enjoy.'

She looked beyond Libby, fingering a gold hoop earring. 'The Dean enjoys medieval history. Giles discovered a fifteenth century Book of Hours for auction next week in Bridgwater. He offered to accompany me, although it will probably fetch a huge amount of money. From internet bidders, you know. Far too much for my pocket. Anyway, I won't be going now. Not on my own. I'll have to think of another gift.'

A slight tremor of Amelia Weir's lips betrayed hidden feeling. Was Giles Temple just a friend, as she claimed? 'If that's all?' The door was already closing and Libby had to step away. She could hardly jam her foot against the elegant grey paintwork.

Thoughtful, she returned to the car. Amelia Weir had gone to considerable trouble to set out the story. Libby could easily check the facts. The Knitters' Guild would know whether the Dean's birthday was imminent, and the local auction house used a catalogue. Amelia had anticipated the need to explain her relationship with the murder victim. However, she'd not supplied an alibi for the time of his death. Libby could not remove either the Dean or his wife from the list of suspects. Not yet.

As Libby started the engine, Angela Miles returned her call. 'Sorry I couldn't talk when you rang. I had an appointment with Joe Ramshore at the station, and he tells me the inquiry's moved on. I'm no longer the only police suspect.' She laughed. 'I'm so relieved. I wish I hadn't bothered you with it all...'

'Don't worry,' Libby said. 'I'm sure hounding you was just spite on the chief inspector's part. He's probably not at work now, after—after the fire. Poor man. It must be devastating for him.'

Angela's tone changed. 'That fire. What a terrible thing to happen. Samantha was difficult, of course, but fire is such a terrible way to go. She must have left candles burning, I suppose. And a thatched roof. Ooh, it makes me shiver to think of it. And you were there, I hear? Poor you.'

'I'd like to talk to you. Where are you? Could we meet?'

'I'm at the cathedral. This is one of the days I volunteer. The library's still closed, but I came to see if I could help out, as everyone's still upset, but to be honest, there's hardly anything for me to do.'

* * *

They found a corner of the cathedral in the South Transept, near the steps of the library entrance. Yellow tape still blocked entry to the library, but the police presence had gone. The organist played something quiet and gentle, and the friends could talk without being overheard.

'I love it in here,' said Angela. 'Even after – you know – what happened, there's a wonderful feeling of peace in a cathedral. I think it's the light. Today's weather is miserable, yet the building looks bright.'

Libby took a deep breath. 'I need you to tell the truth about Giles. I'm not prying or judging you, but if you were more than friends, it suggests a motive for his death. The killer may have been jealous.'

Angela's eyes opened wide. 'I hadn't thought of that.' She sat in silence for a moment. 'Very well, I'll be honest. The truth is, I was attracted to Giles. More than just attracted. For a while, I thought he felt the same.' She swallowed. 'Finally, I had to admit he wasn't in love with me. We were just friends. Giles had plenty of friends. Mostly women. He liked women.'

Libby touched her friend's hand. 'You were in love with him.'

Angela nodded. 'I've been very foolish.' She sighed. 'Giles asked me to meet him the night he died. That's why he was working late. He pretended he was behind with his research and needed to work after hours, and the verger gave him a key. He wanted to be alone with me. He said people were always watching...'

She bit her thumbnail. 'The trouble is...' She looked round, as if expecting to be overheard. 'The trouble is, I didn't go. I was getting ready, putting on makeup. I saw myself in the mirror and I realised what I was doing.' Her voice broke. 'I'd been behaving like a silly middle-aged woman, infatuated with a younger man.' Tears sparkled in her eyes. 'I'm ashamed of myself.'

'Did you tell him you weren't coming?'

Angela looked away. 'I rang him, but when he answered, I lost my nerve. I couldn't explain and I felt so stupid. I just switched off my phone.'

Libby was silent. The police must have checked Angela's

phone records. 'Joe says they don't think I killed Giles,' Angela said, 'no matter how bad it looks.'

'I imagine,' Libby was thinking aloud, 'the police are spending more energy on Samantha Watson's death at the moment.'

Angela dabbed at her eyes. 'So dreadful. Poor Samantha...'

She blew her nose. At that moment, a sharp crack echoed round the cathedral. Startled, Libby glanced up. The noise had come from high above her head. A tremor shook the building, like an earthquake, just as Angela shoved Libby hard.

She fell, cracking her arm painfully on the stone floor. Something heavy crashed to the ground inches away, shattering into hundreds of pieces. A cloud of dust rose round Libby's head. 'What the—'

She scrambled to her feet, rubbing an arm. Angela clutched at her. 'I think someone just tried to kill us.'

Horrified onlookers appeared from all over the cathedral. 'Did – did anyone see what happened?' Libby managed to keep her voice steady.

The verger took her arm. 'I've never known one of those fall before. It's unbelievable.'

Libby looked up at the empty space from which a gargoyle used to leer at the congregation. 'Could anyone get up there?'

'Not any more. At one time, you could walk there, but we closed off the passageway a while ago. We decided it was too dangerous for visitors.'

'There's no one up here.' One of the cathedral guides called down.

The verger frowned. 'You could have been badly hurt. I can't understand how such an accident happened.'

'Accident?' Libby fell silent, thinking. *That was no accident. It was deliberate.*

She brushed plaster dust from her hair and Angela's. A circle of worried faces surrounded them. Two guides, a couple of flower arrangers, one clutching a pair of secateurs, and the verger. They looked shocked, not shifty. Whoever deliberately dislodged the gargoyle had escaped in the confusion.

'Neither of us is hurt,' said Libby, suddenly wanting to get out of there. 'Let's go home, shall we?'

* * *

Libby refused offers of tea and trips to hospital. She insisted on driving home, though her hands shook, and her arm ached from the fall. A couple of aspirin would fix that. She was on the right track. If someone tried to kill her, she must have been asking the right questions.

She opened the door and froze, hitting a solid wall of sound, wincing as Joy Division, Mandy's current favourite band, battered her ears. After a moment of total shock, she laughed. Mandy was home now, so they could talk and clear the air. Mandy could put Libby's anxieties to rest. She was bound to have an alibi for the fire. 'Hey,' Libby called. 'I'm back.'

Mandy slouched downstairs, pale face inscrutable, avoiding Libby's eyes. Libby hung up her coat. 'You didn't reply to my messages. I was worried. Did your phone battery run out?'

Mandy shrugged. 'I was with Mum in Bristol. She's getting a divorce. Dad's gone off with another woman and Mum rang yesterday, in a state. She says she never wants another man in her house as long as she lives.'

Mandy's father had a history of violent behaviour. Libby thought he'd left the area long ago. Was Mandy lying? 'I'm sorry to hear that, but you should have called me. I was worried. Did you go to Jumbles today?'

'I rang them. Changed the appointment. No need to fuss.'

Libby's patience ran out. 'Mandy,' she snapped. 'I'm your boss and I'm running a business. You have to tell me when you take a day off, even if it's a family emergency.' She threw her keys on a table, losing her temper. 'The least you can do is text. In future, when I call during working hours, you answer the phone. Got it?'

Mandy shrugged, sullen. 'Sorry.' She turned away, one foot on the lowest stair.

Libby's voice shook with anger. 'Wait just a moment. I suppose you heard about Samantha Watson?'

'I'm sorry she died. Nothing we can do about it though.' Mandy threw the words over her shoulder.

The hairs on the back of Libby's neck rose. She didn't recognise this Mandy, and the suspicions she'd tried so hard to overcome returned. 'Are you sure you were with your mother all day, and overnight as well?'

'Of course.'

Libby couldn't see her lodger's face. 'The police are checking alibis.' She grabbed Mandy's shoulder to swing her round. 'This is serious, Mandy. I can't help if you don't tell the truth.'

Mandy shrugged the hand away. Her eyes flashed. 'I know you're my boss and I should have let you know what I was doing. I'll make the time up.'

Libby stopped her. 'That's not my point—'

Mandy's furious face shocked Libby. 'I know what you're suggesting. You think I set fire to the cottage. How could you, Mrs F? Don't you know me at all?'

'I don't think that. At least, I don't want to, but you quarrelled with Samantha, you disappeared for the day, and you're – you're different. Mandy, what's happened?'

Mandy sank onto the stair. 'I think maybe I ought to look for somewhere else to live.' Her voice grated. 'You don't trust me.'

'Don't be daft. I like you living here. Anyway, my opinion

doesn't matter. Sooner or later the police will interview you. Half of Exham was in the bakery when you quarrelled with Samantha. She was rude and you were furious.'

Libby tried to speak calmly. 'No one blames you for being angry, but the police will need to know everything; where you were yesterday, what you were doing. Everything. It's their job.'

Mandy glared; eyes narrowed. 'I'll talk to the police when I have to. You're my boss, not my mother. I've apologised to Jumbles, and they don't mind. It won't make any difference to your precious business, so leave me alone. And I'll start looking for a flat tomorrow.'

She thundered up the stairs and the bedroom door slammed. Libby wandered into the sitting room and flopped on the sofa, exhausted. A little later, she heard Mandy's rapid footsteps leaving the house. Fear welled in Libby's chest, like sickness. Where had Mandy been yesterday? And where was she going now? Surely, *surely,* Mandy could have nothing to do with Samantha's death.

18

BEACH

Despite a sky full of dark clouds, heavy with rain, Max and Libby refused to cancel their plans for a walk on the beach the next morning. Libby, still shaken by Mandy's sudden hostility, wanted to talk things over with Max. She hoped fresh air might clear her head. She'd hardly slept, disturbed by dreams of Mandy's angry face juxtaposed with images of Samantha's burning house.

Bear, free of restrictions, bounded along the sand to choose one stick after another from the driftwood left by the tide. Max gripped Libby's arm. 'Why didn't you call me? You could have been killed. Imagine how I felt when I heard about the gargoyle attack from Joe.'

'I'm sorry. I was tired. I thought I'd go home and rest before ringing you. Then, Mandy and I quarrelled.' Tears sprang to Libby's eyes. 'Oh, Max. I'm so scared. Mandy's behaviour – it's not like her.' She gulped, afraid of voicing her fears even to Max. 'I'm terrified she might know something about the fire.'

She pulled her scarf tighter against the wind. 'I've been praying Samantha's death was an accident, but...' Her voice faded. Max had stopped walking. One glance at his face told the truth.

Libby stammered, 'What did Joe say about the fire? It was deliberate, wasn't it?'

'I'm afraid so. The police found petrol residue round the front door where the fire started.'

'So, the killer poured petrol through the letter box and set fire to it.' She shivered. 'He'd only need a match, or a lighter.'

'Or one of those kitchen blow torches. Like the one you use for crème brûlée.'

Libby's breath caught in her throat. Mandy had access to the torch. She closed her eyes, thinking. Had she seen the blow torch recently? She kept it safe on a high shelf in the kitchen. If only she could remember... 'Mandy's leaving the cottage,' she blurted out, 'after the row. She says I don't trust her – that I think she killed Samantha, because they quarrelled the other day.'

A sob rose in her throat. 'It's not always easy being a sleuth, is it?'

Max gathered her close, his arms strong and comforting. Libby clung tight, breathing Max's familiar scent. 'I have to solve both murders, now. I need to discover who killed Giles Temple and Samantha, but even if I prove Mandy's innocence, she may never want to speak to me again.'

Max swung Libby round to look into her face as she dragged a hand across damp eyes. 'You're not responsible for Mandy. She's your apprentice and your lodger, but she's an independent woman, not a child. If she set the fire, she must take the consequences. You can't protect her, and you shouldn't try.'

Libby swallowed. 'You're right, I suppose. In any case, it's not my call. The police came about my – er – accident. Actually, Detective Sergeant Filbert-Smythe arrived, just as I was falling asleep. He cross questioned me for ages, and he wants to talk to Mandy when she comes home.'

'Leave it to the police, then. Tell me what happened yesterday, in the cathedral. You don't suspect Mandy of that, do you?'

Libby managed a shaky smile. 'No, of course not. At least, I don't know what to think any more. My head's like cotton wool. Still, this cold wind is helping clear it.'

Her arm ached, and the quarrel with Mandy had left her devastated, but Max's embrace was comforting. Tension seeped away from the muscles in Libby's back and the hard knot in her chest eased. She yawned. 'I'm assuming the gargoyle attack was designed to scare me away. There's a corridor in the cathedral that runs high up behind the carvings. Whoever broke off the gargoyle must have been up there, but they made a quick exit. To be honest, I could almost believe it was an accident. The carvings have been up there since the twelfth century, so I suppose they couldn't last for ever.'

'An accident? When you've been investigating two murders? I don't think so.'

'No.' Libby took a moment to think. 'I must be asking the right questions, but unfortunately, they haven't taken me very far.'

'The killer thinks you know something.'

'The trouble is, I really don't. I've hardly discovered anything, except that Giles Temple was one for the ladies. He could probably take his pick, from the women who do the flowers, through the Knitters' Guild, to the members of the amateur choirs.'

'Well, you must watch your step and keep your eyes open.'

Libby giggled. 'And keep my wits about me, and tread with care...'

Max squeezed her shoulder. 'Well, you know what I mean. Good to know your sense of humour's survived. And you've got some colour in your cheeks, now.'

'The truth is, I'm finding it hard to sort out gossip and rumour from facts,' Libby confessed.

'Use that brain of yours. Think. Why would someone want to kill both Giles Temple and Samantha Watson? What connects them? If we can find a link, we'll have the answer. You've been out and about, talking to the local gossips. What are people saying?'

Libby described her visits. 'I picked up plenty of scandal from Ruby, one of the knitters. She knows everyone at the cathedral and gave me a rundown on who's doing what with whom. Most of it was just gossip. Ruby likes to chat.'

Libby threw a stick for Bear. Concentrating on the facts helped. She felt better, back in control. 'I thought I'd never escape her clutches. She mentioned the Dean's wife, Amelia Weir. Vera, another knitter, had spotted Amelia out and about with the victim, so I made an excuse to visit the Dean's wife. She wasn't pleased to see me, but she has a plausible explanation for the evening she spent with Giles Temple.'

Max asked, 'What about Angela? Was she one of Mr Temple's conquests?'

'That's why Chief Inspector Arnold suspected her at first. Mind you, half the middle-aged ladies in Wells could have been involved with Giles Temple, by all accounts.'

Max was quiet for a moment, whistling. 'Let's consider opportunity. We know where and when Giles died. Who else might stay late in the library?'

'There's the librarian. I'd suspect him, except he's so small and thin, he'd never have beaten Giles Temple in a struggle.' She thought about the cathedral. 'The place is full of vergers and volunteers, not to mention worshippers and visitors. Dozens of people have legitimate business there. It would be easy to hide until the building emptied, and if you were already inside you wouldn't set off the alarms.'

'Let's look at the detail. Giles Temple was strangled with a chain while reading a book. What do we know about the book and chain?'

'The book was old and full of maps. The police have it, but I'm planning to revisit the librarian. Dr Phillips and I got off to rather a bad start, but I think he may have more information. No one knows the library better.'

'Good idea. While you do that, I'll talk to Joe again.'

A watery sun peeped out between the clouds. Libby loosened her scarf and raised her face to the warmth. In a few weeks, spring would arrive, and then Robert's wedding. He and Sarah had returned to London, but he texted Libby almost every day, wanting to know more about her investigation. She would make sure he didn't hear about the episode in the cathedral.

Thinking of Robert reminded her of Max's relationship with his son. 'I'm pleased to see you and Joe getting along so well.'

'That's your influence. Joe admires you. You've made his work easier, and you tolerate me, so I can't be all bad. He's thinking about going for promotion, by the way.

'Good for Joe. He deserves it.'

'Your son seems happy. He and Sarah make a fine couple.'

Libby made a face. 'I wish Ali would come home.'

'Where you can keep her under your wing?'

She laughed. 'You're right. I'm a mother hen, but she' so far away, and there's no sign she'll be home any time soon. Not even for her brother's wedding. You'd think Robert would be upset, but he just says, "typical Ali."'

'And as if your own children weren't enough, now you worry about Mandy.'

'It started before the fire.' Libby told him about Mandy's break-up with Steve.

Max stopped walking. 'Something just occurred to me. You say Mandy disappeared for the day?'

'On the day of the fire, and overnight. She said she went to see her mother. An emergency.'

Max rubbed his chin. 'I should have realised. That day, I visited Reg in Bristol. He works from an office there and he asked me to review a set of financial documents. At Temple Meads Station, someone climbed out of a taxi and into another car. I thought it was Mandy, but I assumed I was mistaken.'

'Really?' A slow smile spread over Libby's face. Mandy was telling the truth, after all. 'So, she really was visiting her mother in Bristol, though why she left the taxi at the station, I have no idea. Perhaps her mother was picking her up there.'

Max nodded. 'Why didn't she take the train to Bristol? Do you offer such generous expenses for taxis?'

'Not likely. The problem is, Mandy's got a thing about trains. A sort of claustrophobia.'

'Is she getting therapy?'

Libby shrugged. 'I don't know. I suggested it, but I think the idea fell on deaf ears. Still, if you saw her in Bristol, you can provide her alibi for the day of the fire.' Libby took a deep breath, letting it out with a sigh. 'What a relief.'

'Hold on a minute. There's no proof. I can't put my hand on my heart and swear I saw Mandy. The best I can say is that the person I saw looked similar. She wore black clothes, like Mandy's, but she had a scarf wrapped round her head so I couldn't see her face. She moved like Mandy, though, and she had big, heavy boots.'

'Well, your description sounds right. Maybe I don't have to suspect her any more, so you've put my mind at rest.'

'In that case, can we please leave this freezing beach and go home?'

19

KNITTERS' GUILD

The day of the yarnbomb extravaganza was drawing close, so the members of the Knitters' Guild planned to meet on several extra evenings. 'We want to make a splash,' Angela said. 'After all this misery, Wells needs cheering up.' Libby was determined to be there, so she set off once more through the lanes, taking a new route to avoid any sight of the burnt-out shell of Samantha's house.

The Guild had expanded. Several members, new to Libby and all experienced and competent knitters, had added their contributions. Knitted items swamped the trestle tables. Libby, embarrassed, tried to hide her uneven squares, but Angela grabbed them. 'They don't have to be perfect.'

June scooped fingers through the green stripe in her hair until it stood on end. 'Pop them on the table, my love. We're all friends, here. Colour and spectacle matter, but the odd dropped stitch won't hurt.'

Vera sniffed. 'At least they're bright.' Angela grouped colours together, shifting them around until even Libby saw a pattern emerging.

Ruby threw her arms around Angela. 'You have a wonderful eye, my dear.' Angela wrinkled her nose at Libby over Ruby's shoulder.

As the ladies sewed squares together to make blankets, Vera led the gossip. 'I heard about the gargoyles. Now, what do you think? Was it an accident or did Giles Temple's killer set a trap?'

June shook her head. 'In a cathedral. Unbelievable.'

Ruby munched a fruity scone. 'You're so brave, both of you. If it had been me, I'd stay safe at home and I wouldn't set foot in the cathedral until the police caught the killer.'

Vera interrupted. 'I forgot to tell you. The Dean said he'd drop in this evening. He's very excited about our little event.'

On cue, the door opened, and the Dean made an entrance, smiling at each lady in turn, stroking a mane of neat, groomed grey hair. Libby nudged Angela. 'I wonder how long he spends every morning blow-drying his hair,' she whispered.

'Good evening, ladies.' The voice was resonant. Libby could imagine the Dean reading a lesson, filling the cathedral with sound. The effect on some of the ladies made her smile. They fluttered around the room, searching out the prettiest cup and offering scones piled high with cream and jam.

The Dean sank gracefully into a chair, inspected manicured nails, and turned his attention to the knitted goods. 'The Bishop is most impressed with your work, good ladies. He's looking forward to the yarnbombing.'

'He doesn't think it's inappropriate after the murder?' Vera asked.

'Good heavens, no. We need a happy event to encourage community spirit. Have you decided on the date?'

'Next Wednesday,' June boomed. 'Which means we'll get together on Tuesday evening and work through the night, decorating the city.'

The Dean extracted a diary from his pocket and made a note. 'Excellent. Please come to the cathedral after Evensong on Tuesday, for a short blessing.' He turned to Libby and Angela. 'I must apologise most sincerely to you two, on behalf of everyone at the cathedral, for your dreadful accident.'

Angela thanked him. 'No lasting harm done. The statue missed us both. I suppose it will need repair?'

He raised a hand. 'No need to worry. We have a contract with a firm of masons. The Bishop asked me to tell you how sorry he is for your fright.' He'd decided the event was an accident, and there was little point in arguing.

'Now,' he continued, 'to the other reason I came. I bring invitations to a special lunch tomorrow. It's a small thank you for such hard work.' He beamed at Libby. 'My wife asked me to give a special welcome to you, Mrs Forest and Mrs Miles, after your fright. Please bring that charming dog.'

Libby gulped. 'Do you mean Bear? He's very big.'

Angela giggled. 'I'm afraid 'big' doesn't do him justice. The creature's enormous.'

The Dean smiled. 'Amelia, my wife, is exceedingly fond of dogs.'

20

CATS

With so many events crowding into the past few days, Libby had done nothing about Mrs Marchant's missing cat. To put matters right next morning, she set off early to distribute posters. She had plenty of time before lunch with the Dean.

She walked the streets of Wells, fixing photographs of the missing cat to lamp posts. She called into almost every shop near the town centre as they opened, begging the owners to display posters. 'Have you seen this cat?' the text read, alongside a cute photo of Mrs Marchant's missing Mildred. When Libby told the sad story of the anonymous elderly lady who rescued cats, most shopkeepers agreed to help.

The proprietor of one antique shop seemed inclined to talk. Her store was stacked high with brass instruments and fishing tackle, but empty of customers. 'I think I know who you mean. Mrs Marchant, isn't it? I feel sorry for the woman. She looks lonely and I sometimes offer her a cup of tea.' She grew confidential. 'She's gone downhill, you know. I met her at the school gates when our children were young. She was beautifully dressed and, well, to be honest, too posh to talk much to the likes of me. I don't know what happened in her life. How the mighty are fallen.'

The woman leaned on the counter while Libby, keen to keep the conversation going, admired a telescope. 'Mrs Marchant has a son, I believe, but he doesn't live round here.' Libby shuddered at the price on the telescope's ticket and moved on to a blue glass fishing float.

The store keeper continued, 'They quarrelled a few years ago. Her son lives a few miles away, I think, but I don't know the address.'

Libby visited more shops, and although almost everyone was sympathetic, and several recognised her description of Mrs Marchant, none had seen the cat.

At last, feet aching, she taped the final photograph to a lamp post near the marketplace. It had all taken far longer than she'd expected, she was freezing cold, it was starting to rain, the cold drizzle sliding inside Libby's collar, and she was beginning to doubt the efficacy of this approach to finding Mildred.

'Excuse me.'

Libby turned. 'Can I help you?'

A woman in a bulky purple anorak pointed to the photograph. 'That's my cat.'

Libby frowned. 'Are you sure? Her name's Mildred. She belongs to an elderly lady and she went missing a few days ago, not far from here.'

'No. It's Jesse. She went out weeks ago and we haven't seen her since. We've been scouring the streets. My daughter was desperate, but then, Jesse arrived home the other day, all by herself.'

Libby swallowed. 'How can you tell it's Jesse?' This was all she needed – a squabble over a cat.

The woman pointed at the poster. 'You see that white mark on her nose?' Libby peered. The mark was just visible. 'That's Jesse, all right. I can show you a photo.' She pulled out a mobile phone and thrust it at Libby.

It was true. Mildred was, in fact, Jesse. Libby apologised. 'I think your cat's been rescued by mistake.'

The woman's face remained stony. 'Then your old lady should be ashamed of herself. It's a disgrace, that's what it is. You tell me where she lives. I'll go and give her a piece of my mind.'

Libby blessed the foresight that had led her to put her own contact details on the poster. A confrontation between this woman and Mrs Marchant could only end in trouble. 'I'm afraid I can't give you that information.' She spoke cheerfully, hoping to placate the angry cat owner, 'It was a genuine mistake.' She hoped she was right. 'Your cat's been well looked after. Mrs – er – the lady who rescued Jesse was convinced she was a stray.'

The anorak woman put her phone back in her pocket, mollified. 'Well, I suppose it's confusing when cats arrive on your doorstep. I expect Jesse went looking for food. She's always been greedy. She's sometimes broken into my neighbours' houses.'

She walked away, still talking and Libby wiped her wet face. The rain pelted down, harder than ever. *I suppose I'll have to collect all the posters and confront Mrs Marchant.*

Half an hour later, arms full of soggy posters, she returned to the car. She'd never imagined private investigation would be so hard on the legs.

Mrs Marchant threw the door open. 'Have you got good news?'

'Well, yes and no.' Libby explained that Mildred was in fact Jesse, owned by a different family. She coughed, broaching a difficult subject. 'Perhaps you should take your strays to the vet. She could read their microchips. You know, the cat's details, hidden under the skin.'

Mrs Marchant looked doubtful. 'Oh dear, I suppose I should.'

Libby bit her lip, telling herself to walk away. She'd finished the job, and this was none of her business. Before she could move, she heard herself say, 'How often do you go out looking for stray cats?'

'Oh, most evenings. There's nothing else to do now my television's broken.'

The poor woman was lonely. 'Do you know many of your neighbours? I was here the other day and I spoke to Ruby, who lives across the road. She's very friendly and I'm sure she'd love to meet up for tea or coffee.'

She'd made a mistake. Mrs Marchant snorted. 'Ruby Harris? She's no better than she should be, that one. Thinks herself so perfect. Well, she wasn't so high and mighty when she had that son of hers.' Mrs Marchant dropped her magnificent voice to a feline hiss as she repeated, 'No better than she should be.' Libby hid a smile. She'd heard that expression years ago, about an unmarried woman with a child.

'Oh, yes.' Mrs Marchant was getting into her stride. 'Shacked up with a man from the railway, she was. He ran off with a foreign dancer and left the country. I'll give her credit; Ruby made a good job of bringing up her son alone. Then she met her husband. Weak as water, Walter Harris, taking on another man's child.'

She sniffed. 'Of course, she wants me visiting her. She asked at Christmas, you know. Wanting to show off that enormous television, I suppose.'

Libby abandoned the subject of neighbours. 'Talking of television,' she ventured. 'Maybe your Terence could buy a new one.'

Mrs Marchant emitted a noise somewhere between a cough and a grunt. 'Not he.'

Libby wasn't giving up, yet, although it was hard to help this awkward old lady. She had an idea. 'The Cats Protection League. They collect strays. Why not get in touch with them? They'd help you check the microchips and you wouldn't have to pay.' Perhaps the League would find better homes for some of those cats.

She'd at last hit on something of which Mrs Marchant approved. 'I can't bear to think of those poor homeless animals. Someone must save them, but I sometimes wish I had help. It's cold and dark in the winter. A few nights ago, I had the fright of my life. I was on the green by the cathedral, heading for Vicar's Close. I like walking down there. Sometimes, you hear children from the school practising their music, you know.'

Libby often walked Bear along the medieval cobbles of the Close. She understood its attraction. Mrs Marchant talked on. 'A man and a woman were whispering. When I came near, they hid under the archway. I thought they might jump out and rob me so I hurried past as fast as I could.' She tutted, loudly. 'All these people begging, that's the trouble these days.'

'What night was that?'

'I remember it well, because the next day I heard about that dreadful murder. Imagine. I was near the cathedral at the same time as the killer. I said to myself, "Vivian, that could have been you." Made me shiver to think of it.'

'Have you told the police? Given descriptions?'

'They haven't bothered to ask. No one takes any notice of me, these days.' Mrs Marchant was on her high horse again. The mood changes were unpredictable and disconcerting.

'The police don't know you were there,' Libby pointed out.

The woman shrugged. 'If you like I'll tell you about them and you can pass it on.'

Libby took that as a compliment. 'Go on.'

'Well, one was big and fat and the other tall and thin. I couldn't see what they were wearing because it was dark.'

The descriptions were disappointing. Libby tried another

question. 'You said they were whispering. Did you catch what they said?'

'Not really. The tall, thin one wore a hoodie. I remember that. It muffled the words, you see.'

Libby suspected Mrs Marchant's hearing might be failing, but pride would prevent the woman admitting it. 'You're sure it was a man?'

'Oh, yes, definitely.' The old lady paused. 'I'm not sure about the fat one. Could have been male or female. They all dress the same, these days.' She held a finger in the air. 'Now, wait. I remember they had a bag. The thin one handed it over to the other before they split up. The thin one went along Vicar's Close and the fat one crossed over the road towards the cathedral.'

'Really?' Two people behaving suspiciously in the dark, on the night Giles Temple was murdered. Libby could hardly speak for excitement. What a good thing she'd taken on the job of finding the missing cat.

Unfortunately, despite Libby's efforts to help her remember, Mrs Marchant was unable to add more detail. Taking a different approach, Libby tried to persuade her to tell Joe about the two mysterious figures. In the end, she turned to bribery. 'While you speak to the police officer, I'll see if I can find a new television for you.'

'One with a bit of sound. Everyone mutters, these days.'

21

LUNCH

'I'm not invited to the Dean's lunch?' Max lay in an armchair, feet on Libby's coffee table.

'Members of the Knitters' Guild only, I'm afraid. Unless you bring proof of your knitting ability, I'm afraid you're excluded.'

'Just as well, I suppose. But I'm offended that Bear's invited while I'm not.'

'Bear is much fluffier and cuddlier.'

Max stretched out a foot to trip Libby and she fell into his lap. 'Don't mess my hair. I must look respectable for the Dean.' She preened. She'd chosen her favourite bright jade silk blouse and skin-tight embroidered trousers. 'Not too dressy for lunch, is it?'

'You look beautiful. I'm jealous.'

Libby snorted. 'Don't forget, his wife will be there. I'm not convinced the so-called special invitation came from her, though. She seemed hostile when I called at the house. Still, I can't refuse. She's near the top of my list of suspects, though I'm hoping Mrs Marchant's suspicious lurkers are a better bet. I wonder what they were up to in the dark, that night.'

'Probably drug dealers.'

'You could be right. Anyway, I rang Joe, and he promised to pay a visit to Mrs Marchant, and not send one of the team.' She laughed. 'Meanwhile, I have to find a TV for the old lady. Somehow, I found myself promising I would.'

'Typical. Making work for yourself.'

'Maybe, but I mean to persuade her son to contribute. I think it's time he gave her a helping hand, don't you? I'll see if I can track him down. But, in the meantime, I'm off to the Dean's lunch party. It's a wonderful opportunity to snoop.'

She glanced at her watch and struggled away. 'Look at the time. I need to go. It won't do to be late and I agreed to take Angela.'

It felt strange, leaving Max alone in the little cottage. He'd stayed there before, and one day he even cleaned the bathroom. Libby almost died of shock. Her husband had never lifted a duster. Since the gargoyle affair, Max had spent every spare moment in the cottage and Libby, to her surprise, enjoyed his constant presence.

At the Dean's imposing property, Amelia played the gracious hostess, more glamorous than ever in a multi-coloured silk blouse and blue harem pants. She stretched out a hand. 'Thank you so much for coming,' she said. 'I was in a rush, that day you brought Ruby's plant. I didn't have time to chat. I hope I wasn't rude.'

Libby stitched a smile on her face and lied. 'Of course not. And thank you for inviting Bear today. He's very honoured and on his best behaviour. So far.' Amelia pat ted Bear. Maybe she really had insisted he attend. She certainly looked pleased to see him.

The ladies sat, subdued, nursing a variety of drinks. Vera restricted herself to water, but June gulped gin and tonic, drained the glass and looked round for more. Other ladies held glasses of white wine while Ruby sipped from a tumbler of orange juice.

Libby, soft drink in hand, mindful she must soon drive home, settled next to Ruby. 'I'm so glad you're here. I wanted to tell you we found Mrs Marchant's missing cat. Except, as it turned out, the cat wasn't a stray. It was all a mistake. Anyway, all's well that ends well.'

Ruby beamed. 'I went to see Mrs Marchant yesterday and took her one of my sausage casseroles. I pride myself on being a good neighbour and letting bygones be bygones. She wasn't very grateful, but we must persevere with those less fortunate than ourselves. I never want thanks. The deed is enough reward.'

Vera overheard. 'Playing Lady Bountiful again, Ruby?'

Libby excused herself and moved next to June. Amelia perched on her other side, clutching a wine glass so tightly Libby feared the stem would snap.

Bear, who until then had lounged behind a chair, chose that moment to glance through the French doors. He caught sight of a black and white cat digging under an apple tree at the bottom of the garden, leapt to his feet, galloped to the doors and barked at the top of his voice.

Amelia followed and threw open the doors. A blast of cold air rushed into the overheated drawing room. 'He can run in the garden. Maybe he'll stop the local cats using it as a litter tray. I wish your Mrs Marchant would collect more of those animals. They're forever digging up our plants.'

Angela said, in her gentle voice, 'I think Mrs Marchant is lonely and looking for something to love.'

'Perhaps,' Vera suggested, an edge to her voice, 'she should have stayed on better terms with her son.'

They gathered to admire the garden. 'The pond will soon be full of frogs,' Amelia said. 'I can't thank you enough for helping me dig, Ruby. I'd never have managed it alone.'

Vera sniggered. 'Do you keep fish in it? No wonder cats come.'

'We did, but they were eaten. It was very sad.'

Libby thought the lunch party would never end. By the time they'd finished the last chocolate mousse and risen from the table, she felt uncomfortably full. She was tired of listening to Vera and Ruby sniping and nothing she'd heard today seemed at all useful.

The sky hung grey and heavy as the early winter evening closed in. Libby longed to make excuses and leave, just as Amelia whispered in her ear. 'Bear's still having a wonderful time in the garden. Shall we throw balls for him?'

Libby glanced round. The other guests were in small huddles, discussing the yarnbombing. Amelia had seized the opportunity for a private talk, so perhaps the day could still be productive.

She wasted no time. 'I want to apologise again for the way I behaved.' She tossed a brand-new tennis ball from hand to hand, finally throwing it for Bear to chase. Thrilled, he galloped in its wake. 'You see, I wasn't entirely honest with you about Giles Temple.'

Libby nodded, trying to hide her excitement. Did the Dean's wife mean to confess?

'It's perfectly true we've been friends since university,' Amelia continued, 'but we became much closer a few years ago.' She looked across the garden, eyes unfocused, as though gazing into the past.

Bear returned with a well-chewed tennis ball. Amelia, startled, took a step back, hands raised to protect her clothes. Drool dripped from Bear's jaws as he offered the sodden object, and Amelia winced as she held it at arm's length. 'I'm afraid my husband doesn't know that Giles and I had – well...' She hesitated. 'I suppose you could say we had an affair.'

Libby held her breath as she continued, 'I told you I knew Giles at university. We bumped into each other again several years ago. He was married, but I wasn't. I worked in Manchester at the time – in the library.' Amelia seemed to be struggling for words.

'Giles came in, quite by chance, looking for some book or other. He was a very attractive man, as I'm sure you've heard.' She looked Libby in the eye. 'I believe your friend Angela had some feelings for him.'

The sudden hint of malice was over in a flash. 'Our affair lasted for over a year.'

Amelia concentrated on folding the hem of her blouse into tiny pleats. 'He didn't tell me he was married, but I became suspicious. There was a pattern. For example, he never saw me during half term or school holidays. When it came to Christmas, he made one excuse after another, and wouldn't spend the day with me. I still didn't understand. At least, I didn't let myself see the truth. I suppose that's what happens when a woman imagines herself in love.' Giles Temple was turning out to be a real piece of work.

'After that, I followed Giles a few times, without his knowledge, until one Saturday morning I saw him in the park with some children. Two girls. They called him Daddy.' Amelia's cheeks turned crimson. 'I'm not proud of spying on him but at least I found out the truth.' She shot a glance at Libby. 'Of course, you know about following people and spying on their lives. You do it in your line of work, as an investigator.' She almost spat the word.

'Later, I confronted him, and he confessed. He told me I wasn't the only other woman.' She sniffed. 'He wasn't the man I thought. Not at all. I felt used and dirty and I planned to tell his wife the truth.'

'But you didn't.'

'No, I wasn't that cruel. Instead, a wonderful thing happened, like a fairy tale. I went into the local church. It was quiet and I wanted to think. I was very unhappy. Quite by chance I dropped my handbag and a stranger picked it up. That man became my husband. We fell in love and he saved me.'

She blew her nose on a lace handkerchief and gave a watery smile. 'The trouble is, he's such a moral person. I never told him about Giles and I don't want him to know. He might not forgive me.'

Libby frowned. Wouldn't a man of the church forgive her sins? 'You must have been horrified when Giles appeared in Wells.'

'The word horrified hardly covers my feelings.' Amelia hid her eyes behind one hand. 'I spoke to him after a service and asked him to meet me. We met in the pub and I begged him not to tell my husband. I knew meeting in public was risky, but I couldn't have him in my husband's house, and I certainly wasn't going to visit him in rented rooms.'

She gave a sad little laugh. 'I couldn't understand what I'd seen in him. He was still handsome and full of compliments, but he made me shiver.' Her shoulders twitched at the memory. 'Soon after, Vera told me Angela had been seeing him. I meant to warn her – tell her what Giles was like – but before I could say anything, someone killed him.'

She looked at Libby through wide eyes. 'I had no need to kill him. He'd agreed not to tell my husband. Why would he? He didn't want trouble any more than I did.'

She clutched Libby's arm. 'Please, promise you won't tell a soul.'

Libby shook her away, gently. 'I can't promise. I shall Max, because we work together, and Joe needs to know. I won't mention it to the Dean, though, and Joe will only tell him if it becomes necessary for the case.' She took a long breath. 'But, maybe you should think about telling the truth to your husband. After all, you weren't married when you knew Giles.'

Amelia shook her head. 'I can't tell him. I just can't...'

Libby shrugged. 'I'll leave that to you. The real question is, do you have an alibi for the evening Giles Temple died?'

'That's the trouble.' Amelia's face was creased with anxiety. 'I was alone at home and my husband was at a prayer meeting, so I have no alibi at all.'

22

CLIFTON

Mrs Marchant's situation weighed on Libby's conscience. The woman was suffering. She wasn't the kind to fit in with her neighbours, go to classes or join groups and societies. She'd be unlikely to turn up at the Knitters' Guild armed with a pair of sharp needles and several balls of brightly coloured wool. Living alone in a house unhealthily full of cats, though, was no life. Libby had played a part in bringing Max and Joe together. Why couldn't she do the same with Mrs Marchant and Terence?

First, she had to find the woman's son. That shouldn't be too difficult. She thought back to the conversation in Mrs Marchant's house. Had she told Libby where her son might be living? Libby flipped through the notes she'd made and grinned, pleased with her attention to detail. Terence Marchant lived about thirty miles away. She pulled out a road map and drew a circle round Exham. There weren't many places within range.

'South Somerset,' she murmured. 'Wiltshire and Dorset, plus a bit of Devon, and in the other direction, Weston-Super-Mare and Bristol. Well, that shouldn't take too long.' After an hour's research she had two Marchants on her list living in the right area. The on-line census made it clear one resident was far too old to be Mrs Marchant's son. That left just one candidate. Triumphant, Libby set off in the purple Citroen to visit Terence.

She found a comfortable, detached house in Clifton with two expensive cars parked on the drive: a Jaguar XJ series and a BMW 7 series. A handsome, blond god with very white, even teeth came to the front door. Libby mentioned cats and he raised his eyes to the sky. 'You'd better come in. My mother adores those ghastly creatures. I tried to convince her to give them away and clean the house but she took no notice. Now why don't you sit down and tell me all about it. How did you become involved?'

He seemed friendly but Libby wasn't sure she trusted the man. His eyes were very sharp and his lips rather red and full. Not her type. Still, she wasn't there for pleasure. She'd say her piece and leave as soon as possible.

She sat on a pale couch in a minimalist room. No photos or ornaments cluttered the surfaces and she saw no sign of any books. Libby wondered if the room had a sliding wall to hide shelving. She'd seen one in a magazine. She looked in vain for traces of another person in the house. Terence Marchant appeared to live alone.

'I don't want to interfere, but I'm worried about your mother,' Libby confessed. 'She asked me to look for her lost cat, but it turned out it didn't belong to her at all.'

'I suppose she'd rescued it,' her son groaned. 'No cat's safe from my mother.'

'Well, I'm not sure she's looking after herself properly, never mind the cats. There are so many of them.'

'I'm afraid it's her own choice.' His voice sounded harsh. 'I offered to pay for a cleaning woman and have regular meals delivered but she won't let me. Was she forgetful when you were there?'

Libby thought back. 'No, not really. I think she's deaf, though.' No harm in taking the bull by the horns. 'Have you seen her recently?'

He leaned back in his chair, quite at ease. 'I can't visit as often as I'd like. I have to earn a living you know.' Something about his bright blue eyes made Libby uncomfortable. They held her gaze a little too long and his smile couldn't disguise their cold stare. 'Let me get you a cup of coffee.'

'No, thank you.' She didn't want to spend a moment longer than necessary in this cold, featureless room. She forced herself not to stammer. 'I thought I'd get in touch with the Cats Protection League and maybe ask Age UK to visit.' Was she overstepping the line?

On the contrary, Terence Marchant nodded, happy for her to take responsibility. 'That would be wonderful. I'm afraid I don't know what's available for old people once they go doolally.' He clamped his mouth shut, as though he'd let his true feelings show.

Libby decided to probe a little more. 'What a beautiful room.' She resisted the temptation to cross her fingers behind her back. She'd hate to live in such soulless surroundings.

He smiled, unnaturally white teeth gleaming. His skin was light orange, either from trips abroad or visits to the tanning parlour. Pretending to search for a handkerchief in her bag, Libby leaned forward to inspect his shoes. The soft brown leather had been polished to a gloss. 'You're lucky to catch me at home today. I'm not often here. My business is based in London and I'm away most of the week. The train ride from Paddington leaves much to be desired, so I come back to Bristol as rarely as possible. I'm here this week for the opening of one of my shops.'

Libby's bag slipped from her fingers and fell to the floor. She'd thought the name was familiar. 'You own Marchant's coffee shops?' The chain sold overpriced espressos and a range of exotic teas. There was one in Taunton.

'That's me. We're about to open more branches in the West Country, starting with Axminster and Exham.' Libby stifled a gasp as he went on, oblivious to her shock. 'A decent up-market café and patisserie should wake those sleepy little places up.'

Libby bridled. 'Do you think there's room for another patisserie? I live in Exham and it seems quite happy as it is.'

He laughed. 'Of course, that's what residents think. They're always scared of change in an old-fashioned town like Exham. I've done my research, I can assure you. As soon as my place is open, customers will flood in. I quite understand your concerns, Mrs Forest.'

He gave a thin smile, and Libby realised he'd been goading her into a reaction. His research had identified Libby as the competition. 'We'll be offering high concept pastries. There's no need to be worried.'

Libby's head buzzed with fury as she left the house and made her way to her Citroen. The aging car looked small and battered alongside Terence Marchant's highly polished, expensive vehicles.

She rang Max. 'Condescending, calculating brute,' she fumed. 'He'll be trying to put us out of business. High concept pastries, indeed. What's more, he has no intention of looking after his own mother.'

'Mrs Marchant's not your problem, Libby. Let it go.'

'I can't. He could at least pay for her new television. He's loaded.'

'Did you ask him to?'

Libby fidgeted, uncomfortable. 'Well, no. He distracted me with all that talk of pastries.' She kicked a stone down the road. 'I suppose that's what he intended. He took me for a ride.'

'Libby, if it will calm you down, I'll pay for a new television for the woman. It'll be worth it. But you have to promise to stop trying to solve every problem in Somerset.'

'I could kiss you.'

'Then that's my mission accomplished. Come and have lunch. Reg is here and he's dying to talk to you. I'll get Joe to come if he can.'

'I'll be there, but I've a job to do first. I'm visiting the librarian. It's time we got to the bottom of all this.'

On the way into the cathedral, Libby almost bumped into the Dean. He aimed a cool nod in her direction. Perhaps Bear's antics in the garden had annoyed him.

She searched for the librarian. Deprived of access to his beloved library, he'd moped around until someone found space for him in a tiny office, where he sat at a desk, tapping his bald head with the fingers of one hand. His cheeks had faded and shrunk since she last saw him.

Remembering their unfortunate meeting on the stairs, Libby exhibited her most perfect manners. 'Thank you so much for agreeing to see me. As you know, my friend Angela has been caught up in this sad business of Giles Temple's death. She was friendly with Giles.'

The librarian acknowledged that with an inclination of the head, and Libby continued, 'Angela told me a little about the books he was interested in, but she doesn't know much. I don't think they discussed literature. Can you tell me any more? What was his research area?'

'Ah.' She'd hit on the right topic. The little librarian's cheeks glowed and his eyes lit up. 'Giles was a scholar, you know. A real enthusiast for ancient texts. He planned to work here for another three or four weeks, fact checking.'

'I gather his interest was history. Something about Thomas Cranmer?'

'That's right, he was working through Thomas Cranmer's student books.'

Libby smiled. 'They must be incredibly valuable.'

'Priceless, I'd say, although not illuminated like some of the other books we have. Still, they're full of Cranmer's notes, in his own handwriting.'

Dr Phillips warmed to his topic, excited by Libby's interest. 'I'd be glad to show you some of our most beautiful books. You could return under happier circumstances, when all this is over.' He waved a hand vaguely.

'What were the books about?'

'Where's your history, my dear?' He sighed, his tone hinting at years of disappointment with ignorant students. 'They dealt with the old beliefs in relics and other superstitions of the Catholic Church before the Reformation.'

He rubbed his hands. 'You see, in those days, people thought they needed sacred objects to ward off evil. They believed in the devil then.'

Libby thought about the murders. 'They might have been right. Perhaps we should pay more attention to wickedness.'

'Ah, well, we do,' he exclaimed. 'Every archbishopric has someone delegated and trained whose job it is to deal with the devil.'

'You mean, providing – what is it – exorcism? Does that still go on?'

'Yes, indeed.'

Libby moved on. 'I wondered if you could say any more about

the chain used to kill Mr Temple. It's such an unusual way to store books.'

'Oh, yes, the chain. This is one of the few chained libraries in England, you know. Let me show you.' He pulled a photo out of his jacket pocket. 'I can't show you the books themselves as the library's still off-limits, but this picture illustrates the mechanism.' Libby scrutinised the picture. 'You see, one end of the chain is attached to the book and the other end to the shelf. The position of the chain makes it easy to pull the book from the shelf and read it, but it prevents people from borrowing a book, wandering away with it, and forgetting to bring it back.'

'Like forgetting to return library books?'

'Exactly. You'd be amazed at the number of upright citizens with old library books in their houses; books they should have returned years ago. Well, the canons of the seventeenth century were just as bad. Hence the chain.'

Libby pointed to the photograph. 'That chain looks incredibly strong. It would take a lot of force to break it away from the book, wouldn't it? And how would the murderer remove it from the shelf?' She frowned. 'It seems a crazy way to kill anyone.'

The librarian jumped up and snapped his fingers. 'Why didn't I think of this before? The killer didn't have to remove a chain from a book. I keep spares in a box.'

'Spare chains?' Libby's heart thumped. 'Where's the box?'

'At the back of the library.'

'So, anyone could grab one of the spare chains?'

'Of course. The box isn't hidden. The chains have no value in themselves.'

Libby laughed aloud. She'd supposed the killer had planned the murder with care and taken along heavy-duty cutters for the chain. Dr Phillips' revelation changed all that. Perhaps the murder had not been planned, after all. Giles Temple was simply in the wrong place at the wrong time.

Over cheese, salad and crusty bread, Libby recounted her meeting with the librarian to Max, Reg and Joe. She put her worries over the sad cat woman and the unpleasant Terence to one side. 'You see, we've been concentrating on the victim, trying to work out why someone would want to kill Giles Temple. That's why we were so interested in Amelia Weir, and why the police suspected Angela, but perhaps we've all been on the wrong track. What if this isn't about Giles, but the library itself?'

Reg, eating with appreciative gusto from a heaped plate, grinned. 'That's exactly what I wanted to talk to you about. Did you know there's a huge international market in stolen books?'

'Like the art market? You often hear about the theft of paintings, but I've never heard much about books.'

'That's true, ma'am. It happens pretty much under the radar. I shouldn't tell you this, but that's why I'm in the area. On behalf of the International League of Antiquarian Booksellers.'

Libby tried not to laugh. 'Seriously? That's a thing?'

'Sure is. They maintain a database of stolen books and manuscripts.'

'Are you about to tell me the book Giles Temple was reading is on the stolen list? Wouldn't the librarian know?'

'The book didn't come from Wells. It's on the list, but it was reported missing from another library.'

'Let me get this straight. On the day Giles Temple died, a book appeared in the library, from nowhere. No one in Wells noticed it, but the killer knew it was there.'

She spoke slowly, trying to figure it out. 'Giles happened to be there, for an assignation with Angela, when the killer arrived. He was murdered to stop him talking.'

She shivered. 'If Angela had gone to meet him as planned, she could have been killed as well. But why would anyone kill over an old book? It doesn't make sense. We must be missing something.'

Max said, 'All this leaves us no further on. We still don't know the identity of the two people seen by the cat woman, and we don't know who stole the book, or why it matters so much. I don't even think we can discount Amelia Weir. No one can support her explanation of the meeting with Giles Temple. What other suspects do we have?'

'The cat woman saw two figures that night. One took something from the other and disappeared in the direction of the cathedral. It's only circumstantial but I bet that was the murderer.'

Joe mused aloud. 'Amelia Weir could be the small, thin person seen in Wells that night. Could the Dean be the other?'

Libby leapt to her feet. 'I've had an idea. I've been wondering about the connection between Giles and Samantha. What if I couldn't find one because it doesn't exist? Maybe the connection is between Samantha and the book thief. She was a solicitor, after all. She worked with criminals. I think a visit to her chambers is the next step.'

Joe was thoughtful. 'Good idea. We've already interviewed the head of chambers and looked through the files, but no one's found any cases handled by Samantha, other than divorces and a few minor criminals. My men are cross-checking, but it's a slow job and there's nothing to stop you poking around as well.'

He looked at his watch. 'I've got to get back to the station. It's awkward as the moment. Some of my colleagues are like headless chickens. Chief Inspector Arnold's gone on sick leave. He came back in for a few hours, but he couldn't cope. There's no way he could work on Samantha's case. He handed over to another chief, drafted in from an inner-city police service.'

'That'll be a shock to his system,' Libby said, remembering how strange Exham on Sea had felt when she first arrived.

'He's come down from Birmingham with a great record but precious little feel for country ways. Let me know how you get on.'

Joe paused on the way out. 'By the way, officially, we haven't talked.'

24

The solicitors' offices filled the ground floor of a Victorian building in the oldest part of Exham. Painted bright blue, the building overlooked the beach. As Libby and Max sat in a stuffy waiting room, they could see along the beach as far as the nine legged lighthouse. 'It seems such a long time since the murder at the lighthouse. I was walking Shipley, Marina's dog. I miss that crazy springer spaniel, you know, and I think Bear does, too, since Marina went. I walked past her house the other day. There's a sale sign on the drive, and Shipley is still homeless.'

'I think Exham on Sea can live without Marina and her overbearing ways,' said Max. 'What will happen to Shipley?'

'The vet's looking after him. I'd like to adopt him but he's so wild. He needs more training.' Shipley was quite a handful. 'I'm thinking about it.'

'Because you have so much time to spare?' Max raised his eyebrows. 'Maybe I could help.'

'Help? You mean?'

'I love having Bear around, and I have space. Why not find a companion for him?'

'Would you really? Bear would be thrilled.'

Libby forgot about dogs as the receptionist returned to the waiting room. 'I'll ask Mr Scruggs to come in. He's the senior partner and he might be able to help you.'

Libby tried her best smile on Mr Scruggs, a formidable man with a hooked nose and rapidly receding hair. He nodded a greeting, his attention on Max. 'Mr Ramshore. We haven't seen you at the Rotary Club for a while.'

Max introduced Libby, a half-smile on his face. 'This is my associate, Mrs Forest.'

Mr Scruggs looked Libby over from top to toe. 'The chocolate lady, I believe.' The corner of his lip lifted in a smile that was almost a sneer. Libby found the atmosphere oppressive. How had Samantha worked in this place, where women were second best?

Reluctantly, Libby allowed Max to ask the questions. Mr Scruggs would give more information to a fellow member of the Rotary Club. 'As you know, Mr Scruggs, I've worked with the police on several matters of interest to the government,' Max began.

'Oh yes, indeed. I remember.'

'You've been very helpful in the past.' Mr Scruggs laughed in a 'man-to-man' kind of way. 'Now, we're keen to find out more about this sad business of Samantha Watson's death.'

The warm smile disappeared from the solicitor's face, replaced by an expression of well-practised, profound sorrow. 'Mrs Watson worked here for many years and was a most valued member of our team.' The condescension in his voice grated on Libby's ears but she pressed her lips together, kept quiet and let Max do the talking.

'I'm afraid,' the solicitor continued in a hushed voice, full of self-importance. 'I'm unable to tell you much about Mrs Watson's work. Client confidentiality, you see.'

'Of course. You understand, though, I'm privy to the highest level of secrets in my government work?'

Mr Scruggs beamed. 'In that case I'm sure I can help you a little, although I would need an official warrant to show you any case files. The police have already searched them.'

'That won't be necessary. I just want a feel for the cases Mrs Watson might have worked on when she died, to consider why someone might bear her a grudge.'

The solicitor frowned. At least he was thinking about Samantha now, rather than himself. 'Mrs Watson dealt with the more domestic areas of our work. She had a successful caseload including many divorces, people wishing to change their name by deed poll, wills, all that sort of thing, and a little minor crime. She never handled anything of a serious nature, such as murder.'

'Perhaps I could have a list of her most recent clients?'

Mr Scruggs shook his head. 'I'm so sorry, Mr Ramshore. Not even for you.'

'Were there any cases she was particularly concerned about, to your knowledge?' Max tried a different tack.

'Not really. I tried not to overburden her with difficult work. We left that for the senior partners.'

Libby coughed gently and forced herself to sound deferential. 'Perhaps there were personal issues that Samantha discussed with colleagues in the office. Is there anyone in whom she might have confided?'

The solicitor drew himself up. 'I can assure you, if Mrs Watson had any worries or concerns, she was quite at liberty to speak to me. My door is always open to my team.'

As he spoke, a young woman appeared. 'I'm sorry to interrupt, Mr Scruggs. Lord Haversham is on the telephone for you.'

Her boss rose to his feet, face pink with pride. 'Then I must come and talk to his lordship at once. Mustn't keep the aristocracy waiting, must we? Was there anything else, Mr Ramshore? Or Mrs – er... If so, perhaps Mary here can help. She was Samantha's personal assistant.' He gave a perfunctory wave in the direction of an attractive young woman of around thirty, who sat just out of earshot on the other side of a glass partition.

Libby knew her face was a picture of outrage. She'd known many condescending males – her husband had been one of the worst – but Mr Scruggs took the prize. On the other hand, she'd probably learn more about Samantha from the personal assistant than from an out-of-touch boss.

'Max, I wonder if I could have a minute or two alone with Mary. I'd like to know more about Samantha's time here, and it may be easier on my own. Sort of a water-cooler chat.'

'You mean, no men allowed. Feminists only.' Max chuckled. 'Fair enough. You get on with your girl talk and I'll meet you back at the car.'

Libby introduced herself to Mary. 'I'm sorry for your loss.'

'Thank you. It's very strange here without Mrs Watson.'

'I thought you might be able to tell me about her. Did you know her well?'

'I'm just a personal assistant and she shared me with one of the other solicitors, but I've worked for her for a while. She gave me some lovely presents at Christmas.' Mary broke eye contact, examining her own hands. The nails were beautifully French polished and neatly squared off. Libby liked the woman already. Long nails on computer keyboards made her shudder.

'To be honest,' Mary said, 'Mrs Watson wasn't always easy to deal with, but her heart was in the right place.'

Libby wasn't so sure. She'd had plenty of spats with Samantha.

Mary fiddled with a ring, winding it round her finger. Libby asked, 'Is there something you think I should know? Anything that struck you as odd in the last few weeks?'

The PA squared her shoulders as if she'd made a decision. 'It's not much really, but it hadn't happened before, and it was the day before she – she...' Mary's lip trembled.

Libby waited a second to let her regain control, pleased to find someone genuinely upset for Samantha. Mr Scruggs had hardly acknowledged her death. After a moment, she said, 'What did you want to tell me?'

Mary concentrated on her hands once more. 'I think she was worried about something. It started with that business in the cathedral. The – the murder.' She drew her breath in with a shudder. Libby nodded, taking care not to interrupt Mary's train of thought as the young woman said, 'Every Monday I give – gave – her a list of appointments for the week. Of course, they'd often change as the week went on and I'd update her on-line calendar, but she liked to have a printed copy to pin up by her desk.'

She raised an eyebrow at Libby, as though checking she understood, and continued, 'The Monday before Mr Temple died, I gave Mrs Watson the list as usual and she pinned it up. Then the day we heard about the murder, she took it down and put it through the shredder. She'd never done that before. Not ever. She always gave things to me if she wanted them shredded. I'm surprised she even knew where the machine was.' Mary smiled, as though this was an office joke.

'Do you have a copy of the list?'

'It's still on my computer. I keep the originals as well as the updates.' Mary shot a glance over her shoulder. 'I shouldn't really give it to you, though. It belongs to the partnership. Mr Scruggs...'

'Of course.' Libby waited. Mary glanced over one shoulder. No one stood nearby. She typed a few rapid strokes, her fingers flying over the keys.

She looked up again, a hint of conspiracy in her smile. 'Perhaps I can get you a glass of water?'

'That would be lovely.' Mary stood up, touched her computer screen, glanced at Libby and left the room. Libby leant towards the screen, scanning the list of names, dates and times. She pulled out her phone to take a picture, but a message told her the memory was full. She swore under her breath. So much for technology.

She grabbed her notebook from her bag and scribbled as fast as she could. As she copied the last name, she heard a discreet cough, heralding Mary's return. 'Thanks,' Libby murmured, already on her way out.

25

GHOSTS

Reg, Libby and Max settled in Max's study, nursing mugs of coffee and plates of lemon shortbread. 'Did you or Joe find anything useful in the list of Samantha's clients?' Libby asked.

'Afraid not. There were a couple of minor criminals, Wayne Evans and Ricky de Havilland, but neither appeared to have any interest in the cathedral.'

'No links to anyone we know?' Libby was disappointed.

'No. Samantha's clients were small fry. A spot of criminal damage, cannabis, minor vehicle thefts. She wasn't allowed to represent any of the big boys. Her boss saw to that. Both her clients were given suspended sentences, by the way.'

'Would either have a motive to kill her?'

'Quite the opposite, I would have thought. They got off lightly. Joe thinks the judge had a soft spot for Samantha, so he was disposed to give her clients another chance.'

'She was certainly lovely to look at,' Libby admitted. 'Funny, I couldn't stand the woman when she was around, but now she's died in such a dreadful way, I just remember the good things about her. She had sharp wits. She often made me laugh, even when she used them against me.'

She swallowed the last crumbs of shortbread, brushing sugar from her fingers. 'It's disappointing. I had high hopes of a link between Samantha's clients and the cathedral.'

'Joe's team have been running the names through the police computer. They may come up with something useful, but it all takes time.'

'It's so frustrating.' Libby laughed. 'There are plenty of threads, all tangled, like my knitting. Everyone we follow seems to break off. I feel if only I could pull on the right one...'

'Stop thinking so hard,' Max suggested. 'Let your subconscious do the work.'

Bear was stretched out across Reg's feet, snoring. Reg had sat in silence as Libby and Max talked. Now, he shifted in his seat. Bear wriggled and went back to sleep. Reg asked, 'On another subject, has this guy ventured into the drawing room yet? I'd back him against any ghost.'

Max dribbled cream on his coffee. 'Won't put a paw across the threshold. Our ghost still seems to worry him. I sat in the room for an hour the other day and I must admit it's uncomfortable. Cold, as much as anything.'

Libby drained her cup. 'It's broad daylight. Why don't we go in there now and see if we can't get a sighting? Reg, you know about ghosts. You could tell it to go, or something.'

'Not me. I've researched plenty of old houses, and spent the night in some, and I've learned enough not to take them lightly.'

'But things don't happen in daylight, do they? I mean, people see the odd white shape flit across a hall, but I never heard of anyone coming to harm.'

Reg shook his head. 'You need to be properly equipped if

you're going ghost hunting. Microphones, infrared cameras. Or, if you want to chase the ghost out, you need an expert.'

'Dr Phillips told me there are exorcists working in churches. I suppose we could get in touch with one of those.'

Max put in, 'Why would we want to? It hasn't hurt us.'

'But you can't use the drawing room in your own house. Aren't you curious? Wouldn't you like to know why the house is haunted?'

Max and Reg exchanged glances. They were hiding something.

'What is it? You know something, don't you? Reg, you were going to do some research. What did you find out?'

Max moved across to sit beside Libby on the sofa. 'Go on, Reg. She won't give up. You'd better tell her what you know.' He took Libby's hand. 'You won't like it.'

A chill ran down Libby's spine. 'But I love ghost stories. Anyway, you must tell me about the ghost, now you've mentioned it. I'm imagining all sorts of things.'

Reg said, 'It's sad, rather than frightening. You see, one of the men fighting for the Duke of Monmouth, the pretender to the throne in the seventeenth century Battle of Sedgemoor, escaped the battle and ran away, getting as far as Exham. He was a local man, and he made the mistake of returning to his own house, where his mother hid him as best she could.'

'The village was divided, with half backing Monmouth, the others loyal to the King, and our soldier was careless. A neighbour saw him and told the King's men. Informing on enemies could be lucrative in those days. When the King's men arrived, the soldier hid in a trunk under his mother's bed. She pretended illness and said she couldn't walk.'

Libby groaned as Reg continued, 'Needless to say, the soldiers took no notice, dragged the old woman from the bed, levered the top off the trunk and found her son curled up, cowering in his mother's linen. The woman pleaded for her son's life. She fell on her knees and begged the captain to kill her instead.'

Max took up the tale. 'The captain paused, thinking about his own mother. He said to the prisoner. "You hold your mother's fate in your hands. Choose your path."'

Libby bit her lip. 'Did he do the right thing?'

Max leant forward, bright eyes exploring Libby's face. 'You'd expect him to man up, submit to his fate and save his mother, wouldn't you?'

'But he didn't?'

Reg scoffed. 'The coward fell to the ground, snivelling, begging to be saved.' A thought began to stir in the back of Libby's mind as Reg finished the story. 'The captain shrugged and gestured to his men. "Do as you will with her. Why should we take more care of an old woman than her son does?" They tied her up and hanged her from the gallows. This place was built a century or so later for the local Lord of the Manor, on the spot where the gallows stood.'

Libby groaned. 'Did they let the soldier go?'

Reg laughed. 'Not a chance. They let him watch his mother die, then strung him up as well.'

Libby gripped Max's hand. 'That's cruel.'

'The old woman thought she'd saved her son. She died happy, I suppose, though his cowardice must have broken her heart.'

'Is that why she haunts the house?'

'She doesn't. It's her son. He can't leave, because he can't forgive himself for letting his mother die.' Max was thoughtful. 'He's ashamed.'

The story reminded Libby of something she'd heard. What could it be? She screwed her eyes tight, trying to recall the words.

A moment later, she leapt to her feet. 'That's it. I understand what happened.'

He frowned. 'You mean, with the soldier?'

'No, not that. Giles Temple's death. You were right. Once I stopped thinking so hard, everything fell into place in my head. Where's that copy of Samantha's client list? And I'll need your computer.'

She clicked through to the on-line census she'd used to find Terence Marchant. 'There it is. I can't prove it, though. Not yet.' She ran into the hall, ignoring Max's shout, and pulled on her outdoor clothes. 'I'll tell you later. Meanwhile, I have to bomb Wells with my appalling knitting.'

26

YARNBOMBING

Libby and Angela arrived at the cathedral in time for the Bishop's blessing. 'I'm glad you're here,' Angela admitted. 'I haven't been back since that – that thing fell on us.' They stared into the roof. 'Do you think someone was really trying to kill us?'

'It's an inefficient way to do it,' Libby said. 'I see they've sealed the area where the gargoyle fell. They don't want a whole row of statues landing on people's heads.'

'If anything else happens in the building, they'll have to rope off the whole cathedral.' Angela giggled.

The moment of tension broken, they joined Vera, Ruby, June and the other members of the Knitters' Guild. Each carried an enormous bag stuffed with knitted items. They fidgeted, checking watches, keen to get to work.

The Bishop beamed, kept his blessing brief, and let them go. 'I can see you're all keen to begin your task.'

Outside, a cold wind sliced into Libby's face. 'Let's split up,' she said to Angela. 'It'll be quicker.'

'Don't you think we should stay together?'

'We'll be fine. It's a clear night. You go down the High Street and I'll cover Vicar's Close.'

Lights shone from houses on either side, like beacons reflected on the cobbles. Libby tied a knitted scarf to a gate and moved on. Music spilled all around. She paused to listen to a quiet guitar. A piano joined in, then a saxophone. Libby walked on, her feet moving to the rhythm of a tango.

She stiffened. Was that a footstep? She waited, breath held, heart thudding in time with the dance. She took one more step, every sense alert.

Another footfall. Should she turn and look? Libby tensed, waiting, listening. Another footstep sounded, and another, close by. *Not yet. Wait.*

Now! She spun round, arms outstretched, fingers clutching. A heavy object swung towards her head. Libby caught the bag, tugged, and a figure lost its balance, slipped on the cobbles and fell among the pile of knitting tumbling from Ruby's red holdall. Metal clattered on the path.

Ruby, scrabbling to rise, lunged sideways, but Libby was first. She stamped on the knife. 'I don't think so,' she gasped. 'Leave it. It's all over.'

Defeated, Ruby curled into a sobbing ball. Libby's eyes searched the empty street. She shivered, searching for help, but Vicars Close was deserted. Only the invisible music played on, the oblivious musicians safe and warm.

Libby scrabbled in her bag, but before she could pull out her phone, Joe Ramshore and a uniformed constable appeared from the shadows. The constable pulled the distraught, weeping Ruby to her feet while Joe retrieved the knife from the cobbles. 'Mrs Forest, when will you learn to let the police handle things?'

Ruby hiccuped. 'I didn't want to hurt anyone. I was just trying to help.'

Joe spun round. 'Help? Help who?'

'My boy. My son.' She howled. 'I only wanted to stop him going to prison.'

* * *

The yarnbombing had to wait. The Knitters' Guild crowded into the verger's office to drink tea and demand explanations from Libby. 'How did you know Ruby had a knife?'

'I didn't, but I guessed she'd try something tonight. Giles' killer failed to get rid of me in the cathedral, so once I'd worked out it was her, I gave her the opportunity to try again.'

June was aghast. 'Ruby's been a friend for years. She's the kindest soul I know, always looking after others. I can't believe she'd kill.'

Libby, trembling, accepted a cup of hot, sweet tea from Angela. Her friend glared. 'I'm so angry with you, Libby. You knew Ruby wanted to kill you and never said a word. You should have let me come with you.'

'I didn't know for sure, but yarnbombing in the dark was the perfect time to attack me. She'd already tried once, with the gargoyle, and nearly killed you as well. I chose Vicars Close, because I thought I'd hear her footsteps on the cobbles. I'd told Joe my suspicions, earlier. I knew he'd come.'

'I bet he told you to wait for him in the cathedral.'

Libby stirred sugar into her mug to avoid answering. Angela was right. Joe had made Libby promise to stay away from Ruby. She'd have to face his anger later, and Max would be furious, as well.

Angela laughed. 'Anyway, you'd better tell us all about it. We won't move until you do.'

Libby began the story. 'At first, I thought Giles Temple's

murder was about the man himself. He had something of a past.'
Libby caught a glimpse of Angela's flushed face and moved on.
'His murder seemed carefully planned. I supposed the killer
slipped into the library armed with wire cutters, planning to cut
the chain from a book and use it to kill Giles.'

Angela shuddered. 'What kind of twisted mind would want to
use a book as a murder weapon?'

'Exactly. It was very puzzling. Then, the librarian told me he
kept a box of spare chains in the library. That changed everything. It meant the murder could be a spur of the moment crime,
not planned at all. Ruby wasn't there to kill anyone. She was just
returning a book.'

Everyone gasped. June said, 'Why didn't she just take the
book back during the day? And why did she have one of the
books from the cathedral library, anyway?'

'She didn't have it. It was her son, Wayne Evans, and it didn't
come from the cathedral library.'

'Evans? Ruby's name is Harris.'

'Wayne was born before Ruby married her husband, so the
name meant nothing. Her son had stolen the book, and not even
from Wells. From Hereford, perhaps. There's another chained
library there. Rare books are worth a great deal of money, and
there are gangs of thieves, like art thieves. Wayne was a persistent
criminal. He'd been in trouble with the law for cannabis crimes
and he already had a suspended sentence. If he were caught with
the book, he'd end up in prison.'

Libby looked from one puzzled face to another. 'Let me
explain...'

A loud clatter from the other end of the building interrupted
her. Reg and Max arrived, and Libby's heart lifted. Max said, 'Joe
told me what's been going on, and to get over here if I didn't want
to miss all the fun.'

Reg drawled. 'I guess you're going to need help with the yarn-bombing if you're going to get it all done. We're here to help.'

Libby let Max settle next to her. 'I was just explaining about the book theft, but Reg can tell the story better.'

Reg inclined his head. 'There's a lucrative market in old books. I've been working secretly on behalf of the International League of Antiquarian Booksellers, searching for items on the Stolen Books database. I hoped I'd kept it quiet, but somehow I was outed.'

'You're pretty distinctive to look at,' Max pointed out. 'Half the criminals in the West Country must know who you are. News travels fast down here in the sticks.'

June interrupted. 'So, Ruby's son heard you were on the trail of books. He was scared. He thought you'd catch him with one of the stolen books in his possession, so he hatched a plan to take the book to the library. He thought Reg would find it and stop investigating. But what did that have to do with Ruby?'

Libby took up the tale once more. 'Ruby has one goal in life. She needs to be loved. You said it just now, June. Ruby was "always looking after others." She told me her son is the apple of her eye. She'd do anything for him. He confessed he had a stolen book and begged his mother to return it, so he couldn't be caught. If the police discovered he'd stolen it, he'd be back in court, and as his last sentence was suspended, he'd end up in jail. Ruby couldn't allow that to happen.'

Angela frowned. 'But why did Ruby kill Giles? He had nothing to do with the stolen book.'

'I'm afraid he was just unlucky. When Ruby slipped into the cathedral at the end of Evensong, she must have been astonished to find the library unlocked. She was even more surprised when she saw Giles Temple there, probably with his head in a book, waiting for – er – an assignation with someone.'

Angela's sigh was so quiet only Libby heard it. 'Ruby panicked, thinking everything would come out if Giles saw the book. She looked around, wondering what to do, saw the chains, crept up behind Giles, threw one round his neck and twisted.'

Someone gasped.

'Yes,' Libby agreed. 'Horrible. We thought it was a man, because you'd need such strength, but Ruby's a strong woman. She works in her garden most days.'

Amelia murmured. 'She helped dig my pond. It was amazing. She's got enormous muscles under her twin sets.'

Angela said, 'Giles was wearing my scarf.' Head high, she looked straight at Amelia. 'Yes, he was waiting for me to come, that night, but I'd had second thoughts. Ruby wrapped the scarf around his neck on the spur of the moment, I suppose, to incriminate me.'

There was a pause. 'Wait a moment.' Vera, beaming at the evening's excitement and no doubt pondering when to tell the story to her acquaintances, was still puzzled. 'That explains why Ruby killed Giles Temple, but what about Samantha Watson? Surely, Ruby didn't kill her as well?'

Max said, 'I think she did, and I can explain why, although it's only conjecture. Samantha was Wayne's solicitor. She suspected his guilt and she was very foolish. She contacted him and shredded her calendar for the week to hide the fact she'd made a secret appointment to meet him. She's always been jealous of Libby, and I bet she was trying to solve the case first.

'Wayne told his mother he was going to see Samantha. Ruby, thinking Samantha suspected Wayne of the murder, set the fire. She'd already killed one person and I suppose murder is easier the second time.'

Libby added, 'Ruby became totally ruthless. I visited her quite by chance about a missing cat, but she thought I was suspicious.

She must have grabbed a weapon, probably a hammer, and followed my car. I met Angela in the cathedral and Ruby saw us under the gargoyle, climbed up to the passage above and gave the gargoyle a good whack, hoping it would fall on me. It was a desperate thing to do.'

She took a long breath. Two of Ruby's wild plans had succeeded. It was only a matter of luck that the third failed.

June said, 'How did you know it was Ruby? Even the police hadn't realised she was the killer.'

'This afternoon I heard the story of a mother who gave her life to save her son.' Libby smiled at Max. 'The ghost in your house. Ruby once told me she'd do anything for Wayne and I realised she might even kill. After that, everything fell into place.'

Max took her arm. 'Come on, Libby. Let's leave the others to finish the yarnbombing. I'm taking you home.' As they walked out of the building, he laughed. 'By the way, as I drove here, I saw a flashy BMW outside Mrs Marchant's house. Looks like her son's been to visit. Which means, I hope, I won't have to buy that television for her, after all.'

27

MANDY

Max removed the wine glass from Libby's hand. 'After today's success, can I assume you won't stop investigating?'

Libby laughed. 'How can I? I'm just too nosy. I've decided to stop dithering. I'm ready to turn professional. There's training, apparently, for private investigators and I put my name down, earlier today. I'm ready to take the plunge.'

'That's great. By the way, I have news for you.'

Libby's pulse raced. 'Good, or bad?'

'Depends.'

She pulled a cushion from under Fuzzy and hugged it close, suddenly nervous. 'Is it about us? You and me? The other thing?'

'Don't look so worried. You know I want to marry you, but I'm not going to bully you today. Maybe tomorrow.'

'Oh. Good.' Libby frowned. What was causing that tightness in her chest? Surely it wasn't disappointment. 'Can I have my wine back, please?'

'Only if you promise you won't throw the contents over my head.'

'I promise. Now, tell me your news. No, wait. I can guess from your smug expression. It's Mandy, isn't it?'

She watched as Max topped up red wine in both glasses and pushed the cork back in the bottle. 'We haven't been in touch since the quarrel. Not even a text. She's been in the bakery, but I don't often go there, these days. Frank's doing well. He's taken on more staff so all he needs from me are new ideas and recipes.'

'And chocolates.'

'Exactly. Mandy hasn't been home at night, so I haven't seen her. I thought we needed a cooling off period. I'm dying to know where she's staying, so tell me. What do you know?'

'Why don't you just text her?'

'Max, you're wriggling. You know something.'

'I have a suspicion. I was saving it for tomorrow when you're no longer tired.'

'Tired? Me? I'm wide awake. I insist you tell me, or I'll throw you out of the cottage.'

'OK. Reg is planning to stay in the area much longer than originally planned. Wayne's stolen book's not the only one. He has a list of books he wants to track down. He's renting a house in Bristol.'

'Oh.' Libby exhaled. 'That's where Mandy's staying? Where she went on the day of the fire?'

'I'm guessing, but it makes good sense.'

Libby pulled threads from the cushion. 'That's why she wouldn't tell me, because I'd disapprove. I knew she had a thing for Reg, but he's much too old for her. She's had her heart broken once—' Max's hand on her mouth cut off the words.

'There you go again. Will you never learn? Repeat after me, Mandy is a grown-up.'

She moved Max's hand so she could talk but held it tight against her cheek. 'Do you think, if I talk to Mandy tomorrow, things will work out? I miss her. She's also very good at her job and I don't want to lose her from the business. You have lovely, warm hands, by the way.'

Max kissed her forehead. 'Quite the entrepreneur, aren't you? Ring her tomorrow.'

Libby pushed him away and grabbed her phone. 'Sorry. Can't wait. I have to talk to her now.'

'It's past eleven.'

'She's young. She stays up late. Don't worry, I won't call. I'll text.'

Heart pounding, Libby typed;

Hope all's well. Talk tomorrow. Have new idea for chocs.

'There.' She showed it to Max, crossed her fingers and hit the button. 'It's done.'

Seconds later her phone beeped. Max hooted. 'How does she text so fast?'

Libby read Mandy's reply aloud.

Count me in. Luv u Mrs F. See u tomoz.

ACKNOWLEDGMENTS

A great many people have helped in the development of this book and I want to take the opportunity to say a huge thank you.

I've enjoyed many visits to Wells Cathedral, one of the must-see sights of Somerset, and I warmly recommend it to anyone on a trip to England's West Country.

One very special afternoon I met with Kevin Spears, the Librarian. Immensely generous with his time and expertise, Kevin introduced me to the magnificent collection of ancient and valuable chained and unchained books in the library and helped me develop the unique murder method used in the story.

Murder at the Cathedral is entirely fictional and no one in the book bears any resemblance to people I met at the cathedral or elsewhere, except for the famous Wells Cathedral cat who was a real-life character called Louis at the time of writing the story.

The irascible librarian in Murder at the Cathedral is most definitely not based on the endlessly kind and helpful Kevin Spears.

I would like to take this opportunity to thank my 'Inner Circle' of VIP readers who helped immeasurably with reading, revising and editing the book. The word 'verger' caused much head-scratching, as Wells Cathedral staff use the old spelling 'virger.' However, so many readers flagged this spelling as unusual that I decided, with sincere apologies to Wells Cathedral, to use the more familiar version.

I'm very grateful to Chris, Pippa and Nick, my three children, for their unfailing support and uncomplaining willingness to read my stories, and my final huge thank you goes, as ever, to my husband.

MORE FROM FRANCES EVESHAM

We hope you enjoyed reading *Murder at the Cathedral*. If you did, please leave a review.

If you'd like to gift a copy, this book is also available as an ebook, digital audio download and audiobook CD.

Sign up to become a Frances Evesham VIP and receive a free copy of the Exham-on-Sea Kitchen Cheat Sheet. You will also receive news, competitions and updates on future books:

https://bit.ly/FrancesEveshamSignUp

ALSO BY FRANCES EVESHAM

ABOUT THE AUTHOR

Frances Evesham is the author of the hugely successful Exham-on-Sea Murder Mysteries set in her home county of Somerset. In her spare time, she collects poison recipes and other ways of dispatching her unfortunate victims. She likes to cook with a glass of wine in one hand and a bunch of chillies in the other, her head full of murder—fictional only.

Visit Frances' website: https://francesevesham.com/

Follow Frances on social media:

twitter.com/francesevesham

facebook.com/frances.evesham.writer

bookbub.com/authors/frances-evesham

instagram.com/francesevesham

ABOUT BOLDWOOD BOOKS

Boldwood Books is a fiction publishing company seeking out the best stories from around the world.

Find out more at www.boldwoodbooks.com

Sign up to the Book and Tonic newsletter for news, offers and competitions from Boldwood Books!

http://www.bit.ly/bookandtonic

We'd love to hear from you, follow us on social media:

 facebook.com/BookandTonic

twitter.com/BoldwoodBooks

 instagram.com/BookandTonic

Milton Keynes UK
Ingram Content Group UK Ltd.
UKHW020657281223
435105UK00010B/208